# FERAL DECEPTIONS

A REJECTED MATES SHIFTER ROMANCE (AWAKENING OF THE CHOSEN BOOK 1)

CALLIE STONE

As an angel, I have no business getting tangled up with Creatures on Earth, especially vampires. But when vampire Emilio's attempt to rescue innocent witches ends up in his own death, I can't simply watch on. Even though I know the punishment, I bring him back to life, and thus, fall from Heaven.

Soon, my white-hair, huge wings, and angelic powers attract unwanted attention. I must return to Heaven. If I stay, I'll end up as a prized prey of human hunters who will stop at nothing to claim my angelic powers for themselves.

Together with Emilio, I start my journey to the tallest point of the land, the gateway to Heaven. As we avoid my pursuers, I can't help but fall for reckless, kind, and funny Emilio. He might be a Creature of darkness, but he's perfect for me.

Yet with each day I spend on Earth, I grow weaker, and my chances of reaching Heaven dwindle. Even if I make it to the top of the mountain, I'll have to face the hardest choice ever. Because if I'm permitted to return to heaven, I'll never see Emilio again.

Remnant Halos is the prequel to The Angel's Guardians series. Don't miss this delicious paranormal romance read filled with magic, forbidden love, and heart-pounding action!

Download now for FREE: https://dl.bookfunnel.com/ovzzd2h3t1

# PROLOGUE

*"Only the dead have seen the end of the war." -George Santayana*

*Astor*

Sweat stings my eyes as it drips down my face and onto the rough woolen blanket I am using to shield the young shifter. Surrounded by the aftereffects of such a brutal battle, I move fast as I try to escape.

It is a privilege to have the care of the four-year-old Amirah placed on me. The alpha of the revered Blood Moon pack of wolf shifters has given such an honor to me with his dying breath. He pleaded for me to keep her safe until it is time for the Chosen to become.

I step over the bodies, in both human and wolf forms, that litter the blood-soaked ground beneath my feet. Blood pounds in my ears, and the cries of my pack mates echo in my head as someone executes them. I can still hear steel striking steel in the distance. The metallic scent of blood and death gags me.

I can feel the child's body wracking with silent sobs. I lean down and whisper for her to stay quiet and not move. My heart is heavy with the weight of this task and the pain of seeing the fallen. My mind and soul struggle to accept what I am seeing.

I feel the ground rumble beneath my feet and hear a dangerous growl.

"Astor. Stop, *now*," said a deep voice coming from the left side of the courtyard. I know that voice: it belongs to a rogue shifter that left the pack some time ago after refusing to conform to our peaceful ways.

A large man in blood-splattered clothes steps out and blocks me. He holds a sword with crimson red dripping off the tip from his last victim.

"Eamon, I don't want trouble. I'm just trying to get away."

"Get away? There's no getting away. Those who did get away are already gone by boat. It's of no consequence. When we find them-- and we will--I will execute them. Dark Moon is no more, and Red Blood will take over this compound.

"What do you have there?" He gestured to my arms, the small bundle of Amirah still racking with sobs.

"It's nothing--just a wolf pup that got injured in the battle. It's not a shifter, just a playmate of one of the children."

"Right. You always had a soft heart, Astor. You were someone I once respected, so I'm giving you one chance. I can kill you and gut your little pet, or you can join us. Your choice."

I know there is no way I can get out of the compound alive, not now that Eamon caught me trying to escape. This is all the fallen alpha has ever asked of me, and I cannot fail this task. I decide that the best way to hide is in plain sight.

"I'll join you."

# CHAPTER 1

*"Young love is like a raging fire that can't be tamed." -Paige P. Horne*

*Amirah ~ Eleven Years Later*

storm of epic proportions brews inside me, waiting to spew forth with anger. I know not if I will be defiant or let my anger rage, but I know I have had enough of being trapped within these walls.

I glance out the window of our cabin that sits outside the Red Blood Pack compound. Our gabled roof is hidden from unwanted eyes. The fall foliage is a splendid display of golds, deep red, and burnt orange. The breeze blows the leaves off the trees, sprinkling the ground with vibrant hues. I want to feel the air upon my skin and smell the ocean that carries in the breeze. What I want is the freedom to live like any other girl my age.

"Please, father. I just want to go out for a little while. I rarely get to leave the cabin and just look at how beautiful it is. The Blood Moon is coming soon, and you've already refused me going to the Samhain festival of our pack," I plead.

My foster father explained to me long ago that there are shifters that would do me harm if they were to recognize me. My entire existence had been a secret since the day of my birth father's murder. Allowed little freedom, I never get to shift.

"Amirah, you cannot. You know it as well as I do. You torment yourself by wanting what you cannot have," he said.

He gets up from his worktable and walks to me. He rests a hand on my shoulder and gives it a gentle squeeze.

"I don't deny you because I'm being unfair. This is just how it is, for now."

"You always say that: 'for now.' When is it *not* going to be 'for now?' I have no friends. I have no life. It isn't fair." I stomp my foot, shrug his hand off my shoulder, and pull away.

"I'm sorry. The answer is still no. I have to make a delivery of medicines to the compound. Stay inside until I return."

He grabs his messenger bag full of medicines and leaves.

I follow him to the door and watch him enter the forest. He is a skilled and respected alchemist, and those of the pack assume he is a recluse because of the secret methods he uses to make his medicines. It's because we aren't of Red Blood, and he needs to keep them away from us. Since wolf shifters heal quickly and are immune to the diseases that kill humans, his medicines counteract poisonings or for commonplace pains amongst the elders. The pack needs his skills, so they respect his choice to live outside the compound.

Coming out of the woods is a beautiful gray she-wolf--a regular wolf, a predator that migrated to Maine from Canada. Willow. When she was younger, her leg got caught in a trap, and my foster father treated her injuries. Since then, when he's not around, she guards me. She's been my only friend.

She pads up to me, and I let her in the front door. I place my hand on her head, and she leans into my leg, resting against me. I bend over and kiss the top of her head, and she licks my hand. Intuitive to my emotions, she knows I am upset.

"It's okay, Willow. I'm not mad at you, but I think I'm going to go lay down for a while," I say.

As I walk to my room, I gaze out the window, and a thought hits me. Father wouldn't be back for a while, and if Willow thought I was resting, I could sneak out. If I shifted, I could make it to the coast and back fast.

I grab a sack with a short string and jump through my bedroom window, leaving it open for my return. I take off my clothes, put them in the sack, grab the string with my teeth, and then shift. My bones transform, my muscles stretch, and I stand as a large, sleek black wolf within seconds. I run full speed, heading toward the coastline.

I am free.

Air whips through my fur as I skid to a halt at the line of trees marking the forest's end. I stand there and take in the rocky coastline.

I drop the sack, shift, and get dressed as the sound of the waves crashes into the sea stacks. It may have sounded violent to some, as the waves thrash against the eroded rocks of the bluff, but to me, it is a song. I inhale and breathe in the bite of chill in the air, hang my sack on a tree branch, then scramble down the rocks to the pebbled beach where the waves meet the shoreline.

Opening my arms wide, I spin in circles and laugh. The water sprays, landing on my face. I slip my tongue out of the corner of my mouth and taste the tang of salt on my lips. I jump into the waves and dance in the seafoam churned up by the water. I look out into the blue water, feeling thankful for my freedom, even if it will be brief.

The hair on the back of my neck prickles where the loop of my long black hair is tied away from my face. I tune into my senses to feel if there is danger nearby. I sense no threat, but goosebumps cover my arms--someone is watching me. I can feel it; I know it.

I shield my eyes from the blazing sun and scan the area. I try to pick up a scent. With a light breeze, a faint scent surrounds me: the scent of a male. As quickly as it comes, it disappears.

My eyes water from the intensity of the sun's glare. I move further down the coastline. Ahh, *there* he is. I am concerned, but he doesn't move from where he sits on the rocks.

I run in the opposite direction, playing in the water and trying to act natural. I tune into my senses to feel if there is danger again, and I still sense none, so I try to enjoy the pleasures of the landscape. I can still feel his eyes on me, so I turn to look at him. I don't recognize him, but that's not surprising since I'm kept in isolation.

He rises and makes his way stealthily down the rocks. He has a grace and elegance that I have only read about--there is something imperial about him, royal even. He moves with confidence, strong and sure. I can't help but notice he is quite handsome. I shake my head and turn away. This time is just for me.

I dance to the rhythm of the sea. Lost in my freedom, I smack into something hard that knocks me back. Before I land on my bottom, large hands grip my forearms to steady me.

I look up at the most handsome shifter in existence. He is gorgeous. Tall and muscular, he towers over my petite size. Looking up, I see a jawline that could cut diamonds. My fingers itch to stroke his black hair, tracing the designs on the razored sides.

"Are you okay, little one?" he asks.

Lost in his blue eyes, I cannot speak.

He chuckles. "I guess that's a yes." He runs his hands down my arms and grasps my hand. "Come, let's sit. Maybe you just need to catch your breath for a moment."

I am still unable to speak as he leads me to a flat rock. Placing his large hands on my hips, he lifts me onto it. He hops up next to me and holds out his hand.

"I'm Tiernan Tate," he says as he shakes my hand.

I clear my throat and shake my head, my long hair falling loose.

"My name is Amirah Faolan."

"Well, Amirah, it's nice to meet you. I know you're not human; you're a shifter. I haven't seen you in the compound. I would remember."

I blush. I have never met a male before except my foster father's trusted few.

"Yes, I'm from the compound--but I was in Ireland the last few years, training in guardianship with another pack," I lie.

"So, you're to be a caretaker." He shrugs. "Somehow, I doubt that's what will be. Come, let's walk."

He hops off the rock and lifts me down, placing me on my feet. He takes my hand, and our relationship begins. Our conversation is effortless. He thinks I am funny. I don't feel awkward, immature, or scared. I can tell him anything--but I must not. I have sworn to my foster father that I will never.

When the sun sets, I know I have to return to the cabin. Hopefully, Willow hasn't discovered me missing. I tell Tiernan that I must return home before my family comes looking for me. I don't want to leave him, but I must. I wave goodbye.

"Wait," Tiernan calls.

I turn around, jogging backward. "Yes?" I ask.

"Can I see you again?"

"Under the light of the moon, I will return."

He gazes at me with tenderness. "I'll be waiting for you."

# CHAPTER 2

*"No man, for any considerable period, can wear one face to himself and another to the multitude, without finally getting bewildered as to which may be true." -Nathaniel Hawthorne*

I sneak out every week to meet Tiernan. We walk along the shore under the light of the moon with the twinkle of the stars shining above. We spend hours together under the night sky, getting to know each other, holding hands, and talking on 'our rock.'

I never lied to my foster father before, but I now become a skilled liar. Meeting Tiernan like this, I risk our lives, but I can't stop. Tiernan makes me feel beautiful and cherished. Desire controls me.

The week before Samhain, Tiernan tells me we can't meet. He has responsibilities to the pack, and he will be busy with festival preparations, he says. I ask him what those responsibilities are, and he tells me it doesn't matter. When it's time for me to leave, I have to ask, but I don't know if I want to hear his answer.

"Tiernan, after this week, will I see you again?" I hold my breath, afraid that this is the end.

"Amirah," he says as he jumps from our rock and moves between my legs. "Look at me," he orders.

He must know I don't want to because he grabs my chin and forces my eyes to meet his. His touch is gentle yet firm. I look into his eyes.

"Amirah, I have responsibilities I can't ignore. For a week--that's it. After it's over, we will meet again. I promise."

I smile. The next moment will forever be embedded in my mind. He leans forward and whispers my name, then lays his lips gently on mine.

My heart pounds. He presses his tongue against my lips, forcing them apart, and enters my mouth. He groans as he deepens the kiss. Following his lead, I open my mouth more, and our tongues entwine. He pulls me close. He groans again and then steps quickly away.

"I'm sorry. I don't know what I'm doing," I stammer, embarrassed because I must have done something wrong for him to have stepped away. I fight back the tears. He steps between my legs again, resting his hands on my thighs.

"You don't get it, do you, little one? How beautiful you are, how sweet you taste--your innocence is part of your beauty. I want you--but you are young, and now is not the time," he says as he brushes my loose hair away from my face.

"Really?" I ask with a smile on my face.

"Really. Just know that you are mine. Now, get going before I forget how innocent you are."

He pulls me off the rock and sets me on my feet. On tiptoe, I give him a quick kiss and take off running for home.

This is a night I will never forget: under the moonlight, with the smell of the sea in the air, that magical moment. I hold that moment in my heart during the nights apart. It feeds my soul and keeps the magic of the moment alive. It's the memory of his lips on mine that keeps me happy during the time we remain apart.

~

Willow comes to stay with me on the 31st because my foster father has to appear at the festival. I know he will return soon, so Willow and I sit outside around our own bonfire, feasting on snacks and performing the sacred prayer and rituals. On this night, the veil is thin, and those of the Otherworld can come into ours more easily.

When we finish, we leave the fire burning low, snacks and drinks on the ground as offerings to appease any spirits that may cross the veil. I get ready for bed with Willow taking her position as my guard.

I crawl into bed and close my eyes, thoughts of Tiernan bringing a smile to my lips.

~

Autumn turns to winter, and snow sparkles on the ground like thousands of tiny gems.

Tiernan locates an unused lighthouse near a saltwater cove as shelter from the cold. This is further away from our rock, so I have to sneak out earlier. I set aside the guilt I feel lying to my foster father as I flourish under the attentions of Tiernan.

I love our lighthouse. It was once a working lighthouse used to guide the sailors to port. The pack still uses this area to transport, but the beacon isn't necessary. The waves that crash outside make music for me and always give me a sense of happiness. We use a lantern for light and never climb to the top of the tower, but Tiernan does every-thing he can to make sure it is a special place for us. He laid in supplies of food and drinks, blankets, and pillows. He arrives before me and lights the wood stove in the corner of the large room, so the warmth engulfs me as soon as I enter.

More than once, I fall asleep to the sound of his voice and his large hand rubbing my back in a circular motion or playing with my hair. Each time, I wake up hysterical and rush to return to the cabin. It isn't my foster father that catches me; it's Willow.

I sneak out during one of the worst snow squalls the coast of Maine has ever seen. The wind knocks tree branches down, and the bitter cold penetrates through my fur. When I grow near the lighthouse, I shift and dress in clothes meant for warmth.

Tiernan steps around the side of the lighthouse and meets me, lifting me off my feet and greeting me with a kiss.

"Come, let's get inside. It's too cold out for our blood."

We join hands when a loud growl comes out of the darkness. Tiernan shoves me behind him as the growl gets louder and closer. He drops to the ground and removes his shoes, strips his pants and shirt, and shifts. He shields me and coils for attack when Willow steps out of the darkness. I see the muscles bunch in his shoulders as he readies to leap at her.

I jump in between them. Tiernan growls so loudly the earth shakes beneath my feet. He jerks his head as if to tell me to move aside. I will never allow harm to come to Willow, so I place myself more firmly in front of her.

"Tiernan, stop. Please, don't," I beg. A regular wolf will never survive the attack of a shifter. "She's mine. Please don't hurt her."

Willow snarls and growls behind me, willing to risk her life. I don't understand; Tiernan isn't causing me harm. She has no reason to act like this.

"Willow, what is wrong with you?" I bend over and run my hand along her face and down her side. "*Shh*, it's okay, girl."

Tiernan shifts back and gets dressed, never taking his eyes off Willow.

I love him even more for not hurting my girl, especially considering she is still growling at him. He locks eyes with her, not wavering at the signs of her aggression--neither willing to back down from the other, neither of them wanting to upset me.

From that night on, when I meet Tiernan, Willow follows and stays close. Her golden eyes follow Tiernan's every movement. I don't know why she acts as if she hates him. I'm the luckiest girl alive to have a male like him.

# CHAPTER 3

*"I love you as certain dark things are to be loved, in secret, between the shadow and the soul." -Pablo Neruda, 100 Love Sonnets*

inter fades to spring, and I am reluctant to leave the haven we've created inside the lighthouse to venture back outdoors.

I ask Tiernan again what his role in the pack is because, again, he canceled our time together. I don't mind. Who am I to care when I sneak out to see him and lie to him regularly?

He snarls at me when I ask. Never has he acted like this. I back away from him.

"Stop. I'm sorry," he says.

I just shake my head at him, my eyes wide and my hands clenching and unclenching.

"Amirah, stop. Please. I'm sorry. Look, I know you want to know--but now isn't the time. I promise, though, we will talk about it soon."

"Okay," I say. Fear makes my voice tremble. "I need to go now, though. I'll see you in a couple of weeks."

I stumble out the door and run for home, Willow following behind.

Over the next couple of weeks, I miss him terribly, but I don't know how to handle the anger I felt radiating from him that night. I was only asking. Did he carry a secret? Even if he did, I carry my own and weave stories around a fictional life.

∼

Spring turns to summer, blossoms on the trees filling our world with radiant beauty, and as summer bleeds to fall, our relationship continues in secret. He talks about our future, what our children will look like. Will they have my pelt or silver eyes? Will we have males or females? We spend a lot of time in each other's arms. His hands roam my body, stroking and caressing me with a feather touch. He puts his lips on mine, and our tongues entwine, our bodies pressed together. My heart pulses fast in my chest, and blood rushes to my head. His scent makes me dizzy.

"Now's not the time. We must keep you pure," he says as he presses his forehead to mine. "Our time will come, and we will spend our lives together. I'll show you a life you never thought you'd know, and you won't have to think of being a caretaker."

"I don't mind earning my keep, though."

He snorts loudly. "You won't have to earn your keep. You'll only have to be mine."

"I already am yours."

∼

Sand slides through the funnel of the hourglass, and with each grain and second that passes, I fall more in love with Tiernan. We have a love that wakes my soul and captures my heart. No matter how lost within this love I am, I can't shake the feeling that something isn't right. My heart is sold, but my mind has questions.

My intuitive instincts warn me, but I ignore them. Sinister visions of Tiernan invade my mind like flashes of lightning and leave me shaking in fear of the night's darkness. In those moments, I am so thankful to have my protector, Willow, by my side. Afraid but confused, I can't understand why my mind conjures such vile images of Tiernan doing heinous things to others. His touch is gentle, and his heart is kind. These premonitions have to be wrong.

He protects my virtue, and his promises for our life together make me feel that anything is possible, even overcoming my lies. We confide in each other about our hopes and dreams, but I have secrets.

The guilt of keeping our relationship from my foster father and lying to Tiernan about who I am makes me feel sick to my stomach. I live in two different worlds--worlds that can never overlap with the other. I feel unsafe in my mind.

I miss the comfort that Willow gave me and hope she returns from finding her mate soon. Living this lie without Willow by my side, I feel lonely and tortured by who Tiernan may be and not who I want him to be.

It's an unseasonably warm day at the end of February that Tiernan and I almost end our relationship. I leave the cabin feeling the light of love and hope in my heart, knowing that I will soon be in his arms.

I enter the lighthouse, so excited to see him. My happiness falls as quick as a landslide when the scent of another female attacks me. Tears sting my eyes as I watch him jump up and rush to me like there isn't the scent of a she-bitch all over him.

"What's wrong?" he asks as he tries to take my hands.

I move out of his reach. "Don't touch me."

"Amirah, what--?"

"How *could* you? How *dare* you come here smelling like another female?"

He grabs my arm, and a flash of him and a blond-haired beauty spirals through my mind. The firelight glistens over their bodies as she moves her hands up his muscled torso. As quickly as it arrives, the vision is gone. I choke on tears and try to pull free, but he won't let me.

"It's not what you think."

"It's *not* what I think; it's what I know. I believed you. I trusted you. Just leave me alone."

I jerk my arms and break loose, but he grabs me and pushes me down on the floor. I struggle against his hold on my shoulders, but my strength is no match for his. I bite his hand and draw blood. He swears and shakes me, making me cry harder.

"Amirah, listen to me. I've not been untrue to you. It's not what you think. Please."

He strokes my hair, kisses my eyes. He places his thumbs on my cheeks and collects my tears. His lips move lower until they sweep across my lips, but I don't respond. I turn my face away, unable to look at him.

"Please, just listen to me."

I can't handle the pain of my heart shattering in my chest like a Waterford crystal striking concrete. The sharp pain slices through me like a knife. Too weak to break free and too devastated to try, I say nothing.

"Yes, you smell a female--but I don't want her. I want *you*. She came to my room saying she had a problem she needed help with. As soon as I sat down to listen, she threw herself at me. After getting her off, I kicked her out of my room."

My eyes widen at his lies. Does he think I am stupid?

"Really? And why would she be coming to *you* with a problem? Is she a friend? Someone you're close to?"

Tiernan takes a deep breath. He releases one of my arms and rubs at his temple. He opens his eyes again and looks directly at mine.

"She had reason to come to me because I'm the alpha."

I jerk upright and break the one-handed hold he still has on me. "You're *what*? Sure, I believe that the alpha has been spending the last two years with the likes of me." I laugh bitterly. His lies know no bounds.

He stands and reaches into his jacket pocket. He pulls out his insignia ring and holds it out to me, displaying the sign of the alpha on the rough-cut ruby.

"You're... but... oh, my god."

"It changes nothing, Amirah. I knew from the second I laid eyes on you, you would be mine. You hold my heart in your soft hands and my dreams in your innocent soul."

"But..."

"No buts. I'll figure it out. Believe in me. Believe in us."

I shake my head to clear it from the fog that encompasses my thoughts. I only saw a second. He said she threw herself at him. He admitted to letting her in his room. He's not lying--not about this.

"Why have you never told me?"

"I think you have things you've not told me as well. Come here," he orders me.

Afraid he will ask what I am keeping from him and knowing that I still can't tell him, I don't move. Slowly, he moves until he is in front of me and squats down to my level. He cradles my face in his palm.

"Amirah, I love you. You're my future. Please believe me."

Relieved that he isn't questioning me and trusting that what he told me was true, I wrap my hands around his wrists.

"I believe you." I am foolish for not trusting him. I promise myself that I will never again doubt him or our love for each other.

# CHAPTER 4

*"All the world is made of faith, and trust, and pixie dust." -J.M. Barrie,*
*Peter Pan*

illow comes back to the cabin, and it's not long before a gray male starts coming around. Two months later, she gives birth to a litter of pups. Either she or her mate always accompanies me to meet Tiernan. Neither of them likes him.

Tiernan never showed up smelling like a female again, though there are many times he smells as if he came fresh from a shower, which I find odd since we walk on the beach where the spray of the saltwater pelts our skin and clothes. He tells me how much he loves me and continues to make promises about our future, but I still feel that something isn't right.

I can tell that he is having a hard time stopping when we'd get carried away. I want him, but when it gets close to that moment, I feel afraid. He never tries to force me, and for that reason, I love him even more. I still feel guilty ignoring the rules of my foster father and wonder if my own secrets make me feel suspicious about Tiernan.

The witching hour finds Tiernan and I lying together on the pallet of blankets in our lighthouse. I have begun looking at it like it is our home. He runs his hand under my shirt and grazes my nipple. I feel his manhood pressed against my thigh and sigh with pleasure. That is as far as I will go, and it isn't long before the tightening of my muscles relays my rejection to him. He immediately backs off.

Frustrated and angry, he gets up and gets dressed. Shocked at the way he is acting, I sit up and watch. He doesn't say a word to me, and my fear and anxiety grow in overwhelming proportions.

Something is wrong. Something is *terribly* wrong.

"Tiernan, what's wrong? Why are you getting dressed?"

"I have to go," he growls.

I say nothing. I know in my heart it's because I am not ready to give myself to him. I can't. Not yet.

He tugs his jacket on. His sharp movements and heavy footfall scare me. I've never seen this side of him.

I pull my knees up against my chest and fight back the tears threatening to fall. He finally looks at me. He sighs and walks over to stand in front of me, but far enough away that I can't reach for him. For the first time in my life, I know true fear.

"Amirah, this isn't easy for me. I understand; I do--but you expect me to turn on and off like a light switch. That's not how it works for males. We are passionate and sexual creatures. You do not know what I deal with every day: the responsibilities of being the alpha, the pressure the elders put on me to decimate our enemies... I come here to escape, to be happy with you, only to return to the compound each time more frustrated than when I left--and in need."

"Please don't leave," I whisper.

"I'm sorry, little one. You don't get it; you're but a child with this. Right now, it's for the best. I don't want to hurt you, but just because you're not ready doesn't mean that I'm not."

I stand up and reach for him, but he pulls away from my touch. He has never done that before, and it burns my soul like hot wax searing the skin.

"I'll see you next week."

He leaves me there, alone. I make my way slowly back to the cabin. I don't even bother to shift. There would be no joy in it.

During the waning phase of the moon, I worry nonstop. A deep fog absorbs my happiness, and a dark cloud cloaks my life. I cry myself to sleep at night and am short and abrupt during the day, distracted by my fears that I have lost him forever. I am afraid of what will happen when we next meet. It is with a heavy heart that I leave for the lighthouse.

He is there to meet me, and we gradually get back to normal. We laugh and talk like nothing is wrong. We have a meal, play games, and walk on the beach--but he is different now. He still tells me he loves me and continues to make promises about our future together, but it feels like another person is standing between us, not allowing the closeness we once shared.

It makes me try harder to keep his love. I focus all my energy on doing things to please him, and when we talk, I say what I know he wants to hear. He seems to appreciate my efforts, but I wonder, is it enough?

Before I leave, he reminds me I am his and will always be his. His words warm my heart against the icy fear that surrounds it.

It's my eighteenth birthday, and a hurricane is hammering the east coast. We meet in the light of day because my foster father is out hunting his herbs. It will be some time before he returns because he'd have to take shelter from the storm. I leave Willow's pups playing on the rug in my room, and she follows me to the cliffs.

The wind plasters my hair to my face, and a force blows so hard it nearly knocks me over. Tiernan stands in the doorway, his white shirt unbuttoned and billowing in the wind. He grabs my arm and pulls me inside. It takes all his strength to force the door shut. He grabs a blanket and wraps it around me.

"I didn't think you'd come, but I'm so glad you did," he said.

He surprises me with a birthday cake and a sweet red wine that we share by candlelight.

"What do you want, Amirah? What's your birthday wish?" He moves behind me and places his large hands on my shoulders.

"I can't tell you; you know that. If I do, it won't come true," I said.

"Could it be that you wish to live amongst the pack?"

"Mmm, maybe." I try to turn around, but his grip on my shoulders stops me.

"Could it be for pretty jewelry and fine clothes?" he asks.

"No," I chuckle. "I don't need those things. I only need your love," I say.

He places a gentle kiss on the side of my neck, tickling me with the feather touch of his lips, and then moves his hands from my shoulders.

"Turn around, Amirah," he orders.

I turn around to find him down on one knee in front of me.

"Or is it to spend the rest of your life as my mate?" He holds a beautiful opal gem set in platinum with the Red Blood insignia etched into the band on each side.

I cover my mouth with my hand, and my knees tremble. I pinch myself to be certain I am not dreaming.

"My love, will you be mine? Will you let me spend my days as your partner, my nights pleasuring you in ways you have yet to imagine?"

I drop to my knees and cradle his face. I kiss him with everything in me.

"Amirah, you still haven't answered me," he says as he grabs my left hand and places the ring at the tip of my fingernail. Shifters don't traditionally wed in the ways of humans, but the alpha always mates for life and has a ceremony and celebration with the pack so that everyone knows and sees that they're bonded.

"Yes," I laugh, tears of joy springing from my eyes. "Yes, yes!"

"Now, soon, you will truly be mine. Only mine."

I know what he means, and I am ready to be completely his. I stand up, the shadows from the flickering flame in the lantern casting a golden glow upon my skin. I unbutton my shirt. I only hope to please him.

"Not yet, little one," he whispers as he presses his bulge against me.

"Yes, soon," I say as I gaze lovingly into his eyes.

He lays down on his back and pulls me into the side of his body so my head rests on his chest, one leg flung over his. His heartbeat is under my cheek, a soothing cadence. My breathing matches his rhythm. He talks of our future and how happy we will be as he lazily rubs his hand on my back in soothing circles. His deep tenor and the happiness in my heart at how beautiful of a life we will have lull me to sleep.

I wake to his gentle shakes. The freight train of wind had finally slowed, and the rain turned to a spattering. I didn't want to leave him, but I also know the sooner I come clean to my foster father with everything, the sooner Tiernan and I can have a normal relationship--no more hiding, no more secrets.

"You'll come tomorrow, right? We need to make plans for you to meet my father."

"I'll be here waiting for you, as I always am." Tiernan kisses me, then raises my hand and kisses the ring on my finger. "Remember, you're mine."

At the door of the lighthouse, he brushes my hair back from my face and kisses me goodbye. My heart sings in celebration of our love. My body tingles from his kiss, but deep down, I sense something is wrong.

An urgency to get home as soon as possible makes my hands shake, and I run to the cabin as fast as I can in human form.

# CHAPTER 5

*"Death commences too early--almost before you're half-acquainted with life--you meet the other." -Tennessee Williams*

I berate myself for worrying. Surely I'm just concerned about coming clean with all of my deceptions to the man who has raised me as his own. Besides, if I couldn't make it to the cabin, my foster father couldn't, either.

How am I going to tell him I am marrying Tiernan? He will forgive me for betraying his trust because he loves me. I know this. He will see how happy I am, how well Tiernan treats me, and everything will be okay. As happy as I am, I can't shake the tightening in my chest as the wind picks up and the angry breeze surrounds me.

I push my worry aside, and excitement fills me again. With a bright smile and a happy heart, I turn the corner of the cabin to see Willow outside. She paces in front of the door, sounds of distress coming from her throat. Her pups are too far away from her; she wouldn't do that unless to keep them safe. Something is wrong, horribly wrong.

I sway as the world around me spins faster than a top. I lean against the cabin and grab my throat. A loud boom of thunder shakes the ground, rocking the trees. Willow raises her head and lets out a howl loud enough to be heard across the lands. Her mate paces and howls with her. Lightning strikes down in front of me, and in the blinding light, I see death.

I run inside the cabin. Willow and her mate follow me as far as the doorway. Father's messenger bag is on his worktable, so I know he has returned.

"Father!" I call out.

There is no response, so I run to his room. It is there that I find him in bed, barely conscious. He is wheezing heavily, and the rise and fall of his chest are unsteady. Sweat runs down his face and neck.

"Father!" I run to his bedside. I check his forehead for fever and feel the inferno that radiates off his body. I grab the corner of the blanket and wipe the sweat off his face. "Father, please wake up. Tell me what you need; I'll get it for you."

I think for sure he will have medicines to fix whatever is wrong with him. I shake him gently. Then I shake harder. "Don't leave me. Please, don't leave me!"

I jump up and run to his worktable, desperately searching for anything that may help--and then I see it. On the bench sits a box with a glass dome over it, and in it, the rounded leaves and the helmet-shaped hoods that, when in bloom, are the purple flowers of the deadliest plant to shifters. There's no cure for anyone close enough to ingest the dark, wet poison.

I run back to his bedside. "Father, why? Why would you have that?" I hold his hand and ask the gods for help. I kneel on the floor next to the bed and rock back and forth. There is a whine from the door, and then I feel Willow next to me. She lays her head beside my father and nudges his hand. I place my hand upon her head, and I see it:

There had been a knock on the door. My father stepped over Willow and her pups to answer it. He was handed a package, but from whom, I could not see. He brought it back to the worktable and, with his knife, sliced the plain brown paper wrapped around the box and then through the tape. Inside it was the wolfsbane. Panic struck his face. Father yelled at Willow to get out as he ran to the door. He scooped up her pups and put them outside. He ran back and grabbed the glass dome he used to shield his herbs from the chill and shoved it on top of the box. It was too late. He was already being plagued with the effects.

Few things can end a shifter: decapitation, a silver bullet, and this.

"Oh, father, father. Who would do this to you?"

I feel movement.

"Amirah," he wheezes. He struggles to draw oxygen into his lungs.

"*Shh*, father. Don't talk," I cry. I try to still him, but he is restless.

Weak and shaking, he whispers, "Amirah, from your father, through me, to you. You're *the One*." He coughs, and a gurgling emerges from deep in his throat, the agony clear on his face.

I feel his body growing colder with each rasp. Uncontrollable sobs tear themselves from my throat. He moves his hand toward mine and forces something cold and hard into my hand.

With his last breath, a radiant blue light encompasses the room. The brightness blinds me with its brilliant illumination. My hand pulses like a beating heart. I open my fingers, and the amulet drops onto the bed. The palm of my hand holds the mark of the crescent moon.

My mind and heart race, both gripped tightly in the clutches of grief. The crescent moon in my palm pulses, emitting rays of light.

What does this mean? Why did this happen? Who would want to kill my kind and generous foster father? Am I next?

Seized by confusion and fear, I don't know what to do. I have nowhere to go and no one to help me--except Tiernan. He will help me.

I order Willow to guard and shift in motion, leaving my clothes to lay in a shredded pile of fabric. I raise my head and howl. My grief, fear, and anger reverberate and cause the trees around me to shake. Lightning strikes high in the sky, and thunder joins its cadence with my sound.

My pain engulfs me in its powerful ache.

~

*On Moonstone Island*

Moonstone Island is the home of the shifters who survived the attack on Dark Moon fourteen years ago. Under the rule of the fallen alpha's second-in-command, they have built a new life.

The restless sea protects the island for as far as the naked eye can reach. The jagged formations of the cliffs create a treacherous border. The haven they've created is secure from the prying eyes of humans and unwanted battles so that they can live in peace.

The traditional stone mansion sits atop the highest point, and inside those impenetrable walls, Malachi Lycidas, the alpha, sits in his library by the stone fireplace. Cold air seeps into the room, drawing Malachi's attention away from his book. He gets up to check the window in his office when he sees a blue light shining from under the panel to the secret space hidden within the walls.

With trepidation in his step, he moves to the panel. The light grows brighter. He finds the spot to release the panel, and it swings open with an eerie creak from the rusty hinges. Inside, on the top tier of the red felted stand, sits the crown of the Chosen. The platinum 'V' gleams brightly from the gems. Intricately engraved phases of the moon grace each side. Breathtaking in its beauty, it has a heartbeat of its own. The magical blue illuminations drown the room with their radiance.

He runs to the door and calls for the councilmen to come at once. In the rays of the gleaming light, he slumps into the nearest chair.

The councilmen rush through in a wave of panic; he's never called for them like this before. The brilliance of the light blinds their vision. Lorcan, the youngest but also the head of the council, steps forward. His devotion to the pack is strong. He places his hand on his short dagger in its leather sheath at his hip, ready to defend his pack if needed. He asks, "What is this, Malachi?"

Malachi waves his hand at the panel door. Four heads turn, eyes locked on the crown that hums with vitality.

"It is time. The Chosen is near, and it's time," Malachi says.

Lorcan goes to the door and calls for Blade Marrock, the fiercest warrior, the most feared member of their pack. In seconds, his seven-foot-tall frame of bulky muscle stands in the doorway. His hand rests on his longsword, his eyebrows arched in curiosity.

Malachi stands and faces him, staring hard at Blade to convey the seriousness of what he is about to say. "The time has come," he says. "Are you ready to accept your duty, above and beyond your allegiance to the pack?"

Blade nods. "I am. I've trained for this my entire life. I will do what needs to be done."

"Gather your top men. We will meet soon," Malachi says.

Blade nods again and leaves the room as loudly as he arrived.

"Lorcan, prepare." Malachi looks at all of the councilmen one by one. "Everyone must prepare, for this is the start of the battle of all battles, and we must win, or our ways will cease."

Malachi wipes sweat from his forehead and notices his hands shaking. "It is time," he whispers.

# CHAPTER 6

*"Now, by mine honour, by my life, my troth, I will appeach the villain." -*
*William Shakespeare, Julius Caesar*

I run to the compound, plowing through the shifters unfortunate enough to get in my path. Finally, I enter the mansion and catch my breath. I follow Tiernan's scent to an intricately carved pine door. I shove my body into it--once, twice, then the wood splinters, and the door swings open.

Tiernan jumps from his seat. Seeing that it is me, his eyes grow wide in alarm. He orders everyone out of the room as soldiers rush in, ready for attack. With a wave of his hand, he sends them out.

I shift, my muscles change, my bones creak as they're reformed. The pain is subtle but less than I expected from shifting twice so close together. I rise to human form and stand there, naked and shivering. Tiernan grabs his jacket off the back of his chair and wraps it around me.

"Amirah, what's wrong?" he asks. He rubs his hands up and down my arms.

Unable to speak and overwhelmed by the varied emotions running through my mind and heart, I just stand there. He walks me over to the fireplace, shushing me, and tells me to calm down.

"My father…"

"*Shh*, he will come around," Tiernan says, assuming this is about our betrothal. I shake my head, still crying.

I fight to breathe. I squeeze my eyes shut and try to calm myself. My teeth chatter like the bones of a skeleton rattling in the wind.

"My father--he's gone. He was murdered."

"*What?*"

"When I got back, my father was in bed, barely breathing from wolfsbane poison exposure. It was murder. He's dead!" I wail.

Tiernan's eyes narrow as he looks at me closely. I am so overcome with grief; my senses aren't strong, and my intuitions are down. I should feel danger.

"Is that all?" he asks.

I sniffle and hiccup.

He grabs my shoulders again, his grip harsh.

"Amirah, answer me."

I take another deep breath, calm my racing heart. "There's this." I hold my hand palm up and show him the crescent moon.

Uncontrollable rage washes over him. It happens so fast that I jump in surprise. He shakes me so violently that my organs bounce around in my body. Weak from the rapid shifts and the run to the cabin, I have no strength to break his hold.

"You traitorous bitch!" he yells. "Oh, you will pay. Where's the amulet?"

He slams me up against the wall hard enough to shake the shelves. Books crash to the floor. "I said where is the amulet!" he yells, so close to my face, hot gusts of breath heat my cold skin.

Unable to believe that this is my fiancé, my Tiernan, I say nothing. This must be a nightmare; it *must* be.

He grabs a knife off his desk and places the tip on the right side of my neck. "I'll ask you once more: *where* is the amulet?"

"I don't have it with me," I squeak.

He growls deep in his throat. His teeth clench, and blue-green veins pop out on his temples. His hands grip me tightly enough that his nails dig through the fabric of his jacket and into my skin.

"I left it. I came straight here for help. Please," I sniffle.

"*Help* you?" He chuckles cruelly, then throws his head back and howls with a ferocity that only alphas have.

Running feet thump on the floor. Someone enters the room, but I can't see past Tiernan to see who it is.

"Take her to the tower room. She'll be put to death."

"Tiernan!" I scream. "Tiernan, please! I love you!"

His face distorts, and a cruel sneer forms across his lips. He laughs loudly.

"Yeah, well, Amirah, only the foolhardy actually fall in love." He motions to the hulking male.

Rough hands grab me. I fight against it. I pull and twist my body away.

"Come on, bitch," growls a voice I find familiar but unable to place. I feel myself being lifted into the air, as if I weigh as little as a pillow, and tossed over his shoulder. He swoops to grab the jacket that slipped off me and throws it over my nakedness. I rake my nails along his back and draw blood.

"Do it again, and I'll cut you." He reaches up and yanks my hair hard enough my head snaps up.

"Stop," orders Tiernan.

He walks up to me and runs a fingernail down my cheek as I hang upside down. "I must say, I can't regret the time I spent with you. You see, my dear, *you* are why I found your foster father. I was looking for you when I discovered his traitorous activities. So, my dear, it is because of you he is dead."

Anger courses through my body. I struggle and scratch to no avail.

"Oh--and Eamon," Tiernan says.

Eamon turns to look at him.

"If she fights, cut her, but don't kill her. When it's time, after I take her--*then* you can."

He laughs viciously and leaves the room. I stop fighting. I am afraid that Eamon really will cut me.

A door opens, and he carries me into a room shrouded in darkness. Eamon dumps me onto the cold, hard ground. My head cracks off the floor, and a wave of nausea hits me. He yanks me up by my throat with one hand and runs his other hand along the side of my breast. I gag at his touch, vomit pooling in the back of my throat.

"Maybe *I* will take you. I like it rough, and I doubt Tiernan would care if I harmed you in the taking."

I recoil at his words. He gives me another shove, and I lose my balance. I crash to the cold, hard, concrete floor and smack my face. My cheek stings, and my vision blurs. I struggle to stay conscious as darkness shrouds me like a fog rolling across the sea.

The long wooden table stretches the length of the room. In the high-back chairs that surround it sit the councilmen. Blade stands guard at the door, his stance strong. The pack seer is in the light of the rising sun on the opposite side of the room. Her long, curly red hair and midnight-blue gown billow in the wind. The room vibrates with magic. Lorcan leans back in his chair and watches me thump my finger repetitively on the tabletop. Finally, the seer speaks.

"The Chosen is near, in the Dark Moon origin. The top points to the light. Great harm will come to her should you fail. Her heart bleeds, her soul weeps, and her strength wanes."

She looks at Blade. "Through the tower, you go--the passage of the side, the winding stairs, her body you will find. Take men to protect and travel through the dark waters under the first quarter moon. It must be you." She closes her eyes and then opens them. The wind calms; her gown settles.

"Uh," Lorcan clears his throat. "Thank you, Serenity. You have served us well."

Blade steps forward to escort her from the room.

"Have Caleb escort her back, Blade. I think we need to talk," Lorcan says.

"Yes, yes--do that, then sit with us," I say.

Blade opens the door and gestures for Caleb, a young soldier and his protege. He tells him to escort Serenity to her home, then return to his post. He strides to the table with a casual arrogance and takes the only vacant seat.

"Riddle me this. What the hell was she talking about?" says Killian, my son.

"I think…" Lorcan pauses and reviews her words in his mind. "Blade must go to the compound the night of the quarter moon, that's tomorrow, and go through a hidden door in the tower and get her. She said it must be you, so…" he says and shrugs his shoulders. "Does anyone know where the door is?" he asks the room at large.

"I do," I say. "It's in the northwest, marked by a black moon in the stone etchings. If you feel with your fingertips, you'll find the latch. I've never been inside, though, so I do not know what you'll face."

Blade shrugs, not disturbed by the unknown.

The journey to the compound takes time to arrange. Blade gathers his men and prepares for their departure. I stop him at the hidden dock between two towering cliffs.

"Blade, don't engage in battle. You are under-manned. Their soldiers are large in numbers. Just get her and get back here. I know you; you'll want to fight. That time will come, but it is not now. Just *get her back here.*"

Blade nods his acknowledgment--though if a battle comes to him, I know Blade will fight.

# CHAPTER 7

*"Years of love have been forgot, in the hatred of a minute." -Edgar Allan Poe*

I sit on the floor in total darkness and press my back against the wall. Tiernan's jacket is the only thing that separates my body from the rough, cold stones. I lost my father--I lost *both* my fathers--and the one who held my heart in his hands destroyed me.

Afraid and helpless, I rock back and forth to seek solace from the motion. There must be a way to escape, but even if I do, where would I go? Surely the cabin isn't safe anymore, and I have no one to turn to.

I hear the voices of two women outside the door, but I can't make out what they are saying.

There is a thump, then a high-pitched screech. The door opens, and a woman dressed in servants' clothes walks in. Her plain beige tunic hangs from her body, and the cheap fabric makes a scratchy sound when she moves. Her pants look well worn below the hem of the apron tied around her waist. The apron is spotless, while the rest is drab and old.

I know she must be low in the pack order. She holds a lantern and a brown sack. I eye the door, wondering if I have the strength to push past her or move fast enough to go around her. She must be able to read my thoughts because she slams the door shut behind her.

"Don't even think about it. If ya go out there, you'll have bigger things to worry about. Gia wants a piece of ya. That's why Tiernan ordered me to watch ya n'stead of her. He said your face mustn't be marked, so your beauty is there for all to see when you are laid upon the sacrificial altar, and Gia wants to scratch yer eyes out," she rambles.

I say nothing. I can't even think straight, and her babbling makes my head pound more.

"Oh, I'm Emma. No need to tell me who ya are. We all know, Amirah. Heard you took some skin out of Eamons' back. You got some fight in ya. Not smart of you, as he's to be your executioner and can make it unpleasant, but still, ya got some fight."

My eyes move to the door again as Emma empties the bag onto the floor next to me. A pair of trousers, boots, a tunic shirt, and undergarments tumble out. I look at the pile in distaste. I wonder who it belonged to and if it's clean. The absurdity that I think of such things at a time like this while I sit here naked doesn't escape me.

She puts food and water on the table in the corner. I think again about making a run for it.

She watches me. "Go ahead. Gia is out there, and she won't think twice about gutting yer belly and pulling yer insides out."

I look at Emma. "Why does she hate me so badly?"

Emma's eye twitches. "Do ya really not know?"

"Know what?"

Emma cackles like a witch. "She was to mate Tiernan until he found ya. After that, she was good enough for his bed, but he wouldn't wed her."

My thoughts go back to the premonition I had of him and the woman in his room. "The blonde."

Emma cocks her head to the side and looks at me inquisitively.

"I saw a vision, a premonition, of Tiernan and a blonde being intimate--but when I questioned him about it, he said she came to him under false pretenses and threw herself at him. He said he kicked her out of his room--that he didn't want her, he wanted me."

Emma snorts loudly. "Yep, he kicked her out, all right--every mornin' after shaggin' her all night long. Since that's all he wanted her for after he met ya, she wants to kill ya. Still, even though she knew he found 'nother, she climbed into his bed. She got what she deserved to my way of thinkin'. Guess they can mate now since you'll be dead," she states as casually as if she is discussing the weather or crop rotation.

I can't stop it; a tear slowly leaks from my eye. My vision was true. My heart was his, but his was never mine. I hate myself. The realization fills me with self-loathing, and regret slams into my stomach like an iron fist.

Emma pats my hand awkwardly.

"What's to become of me?" I ask.

"Well, Tiernan is planning a grand sacrificial ceremony on yer behalf, with all the pack there. Yer beauty n grace on the altar for all to see, he says. Then Eamon will put you to death. I heard he's quick, but he's a mite pissed at you for scratchin' up his back, so I'm thinkin' he may make ya suffer."

I gulp. "When is this to happen?"

"In two days' time, it'll all be over. Get dressed and eat. I won't be letting Gia in, so don't ya worry none. I'll check on ya later tonight."

Emma leaves the room and, with a click, locks me inside. My hurting heart and tortured mind are my only company.

Hours pass as I stare into the darkness, though I don't know how many. I mourn my foster father's death, and the betrayal of Tiernan fills my waking thoughts.

I force myself to move. I notice a window high up. I circle the tower in search of a way to reach it, though what I would do if I got up there, I do not know. I suppose I could throw myself out the window and hope I die in the fall--at least then my death wouldn't be part of a sacrifice.

I find no sturdy furniture in the room and nothing with enough height to reach the window. I run my hands along the wall under the pane and hope to find ledges large enough I can use as a foothold. There is nothing; the ridges are tiny and sharp like miniature blades. I give up and lay down on the blanket that Emma left.

Sometime later, I hear the door click and sit up.

"Hiya. I brought ya a meal, and I thought ya might be bored, so I brung 'nother lantern and a book," Emma says.

"A *book*? I'm to be executed, my father is dead, the love of my life is a beast, and you want me to read a book?"

"Well, ya can't change anythin'. Oh, and just so's ya know, Tiernan went to your cabin in search of the amulet. He couldn't find it. Heard ya pa's body was gone, too. He's in a fit over it and says he's gonna beat it out of ya tonight. He said he'd have a taste of ya then torture ya 'til you tell him where to find the amulet," she says.

"But I don't know what happened after I left. I came straight to Tiernan. I thought he would help me, comfort me."

Emma's jaw drops. "Help you? Comfort you? He is cruel 'n full of bloodthirst. He helps 'n comforts no one. Sure, he's got a kindness for ya, cus he has ya up here n'stead of being tortured and has me givin' ya food 'n drink. He told the soldiers not to touch ya. He usually lets them amuse themselves with the female captives until they beg' fer death--but not you."

I cast my eyes down. "I thought he loved me. He told me he did. He asked me to mate."

"Well, maybe he cares a bit. I doubt it, but if it makes ye feel better thinkin' it, I see no harm since signs are there. Fact is, he needed ya. I hear he told his friends the day he met ya, he knew he would hunt ya until you were his, that somethin' told him it had to be. I'm sorry, girl, but love ain't somethin' he can feel. Tiernan's feared far 'n wide, not known to havin' emotions, like." She pats my hand in comfort. "Males plain suck--'specially here. I hate it here. Someday, I'll get away from all this."

I wonder why she uses ten sentences to say what could easily be said in three, then I scold myself.

"I'm so stupid. I... I think he killed my foster father--at least, that's what he said--or ordered someone to give him the wolfsbane. I can't believe this is the male I fell in love with." I take a deep breath. "I believed in him."

"Well, now, you ain't the first girl he's played, and you ain't gonna be the last, neither." She looks me in the eye. "I'm gonna tell ya how it is: he knew your foster pa was betrayin' him--and he killed your birth pa with his own sword a long time ago. Tiernan, he loves to kill. He lives fer it. I'm surprised he's not killin' ya himself."

She gets up and gathers Tiernan's jacket and the dishes of leftover food from earlier. "I'm not s'posed to come in here unless it's ta check on ya and deliver, but I'll sneak in later tonight. We can have some girl-talk, and I'll tell ya what I know. At least ya can die with no ques-tions," she says.

"Why are you being nice to me?"

"'Cuz I feel bad fer ya, and 'cuz I was one of the girls he lied to, too--but I'm stuck here, ya see. Tiernan, he don't let us leave the compound."

She leaves, and I curl up on the blanket again, the food and book untouched.

~

Emma comes back, but I've lost all semblance of time. I sit up and run my hands down my face. Emma sits down on the blanket next to me.

"Ya really thought he loved ya, huh?" she asks.

I nod. "I did. I was foolish and ignored signs I shouldn't have. I betrayed my foster father, and my lies and actions led to his death."

"Yup, we females are dumb like that with males. I once believed him, too, though anyone who looks at him can see he ain't nuthin' but pure evil. But ya can't be blamin' yerself for your foster father's death. Tiernan knew there was a traitor in the pack long before." She waves her hands at me. "He was narrowin' it down. It wasn't yer fault," she said. It woulda happened anyway. Yer death would happen anyway, too, no matter."

There's a scuffle in the hall, and we strain to listen. Right outside the door, we hear a series of thumps that has Emma reaching for the knife hidden in the folds of her apron. The gleam of the lantern highlights the sharp silver tip. I have no weapon to protect myself.

We hear Gia screaming and the deep voice of a male. "Come on, Gia. You know you are not to be here. If Tiernan finds out that you are ignoring his orders, he will be pissed as hell."

"I don't care if he's mad or not; that bitch is *mine*. I deserve to be allowed to gut her!" Gia yells.

"You'll care when he takes another to his bed--and you *know* he will. He's already taught you that lesson. Come on, now; I don't want to hurt you. Just come along."

There's a dragging sound. "I'll get you yet, you bitch," sounds through the door, and then it's quiet--for a millisecond.

"She must have been tryin' to get to ya again. Girl, I'm telling ya, if she gets hold of ya, you ain't gonna have to worry about Eamon. But I can take her, and I got my orders from Tiernan to not let her near ya." Emma snickers. "We all got those orders.

"I gotta go. I'll see ya in the mornin' ta get ya ready. At least you'll be pretty when you die."

She gets up and checks the hall before she slips through the tiny crack of the doorway.

Numbness sets in. My brain hurts. My body is weak. I lay down and wrap myself in the blanket, and drift off to sleep.

Venomous snakes fill my dreams; the tongues of vipers slash at me. Each snake bears the sign of Red Blood, and their only goal is to end me.

# CHAPTER 8

*"There is always fear of the unknown." -Berhan Ahmed*

A heavy, scraping sound wakes me from my nightmare. The lantern went out while I slept, so I hold still and give my eyes time to adjust.

Across the room, concrete shifts, and the largest male I have ever seen stands in the opening. He reaches his arm out and waves his fingers for me to come.

I scurry as far away as I can. I shake my head. I open my mouth to scream when he pulls an ax from behind him. Fear silences me. He waves his fingers at me again, beckoning me to go to him.

"What the hell," he mutters and makes quick work of crossing the room. "Do not make a sound. I am not here to hurt you. You need to come with me," he whispers.

I still don't move, so he picks me up and carries me away like a sack of potatoes. Once through the opening, he sets me down on the stairs. Cobwebs fill the space; the scurry of critters is the only sound. He keeps one hand wrapped around my arm.

"I'm Blade Marrock, and I'm from your father's pack. I'm here to save you, but you must come with me." Relief washes over me, and I nod.

I follow him down the stairs as quickly as I can in the dark. Along the way, we meet others who greet us with nods and hand signals. "We must go quickly to the boat--careful to remain unseen, silent in the night. If we get separated, get out. Just get away; I'll find you."

"Wait," Emma's voice startles me. My rescuer shoves me behind him, his ax at the ready. "Please, take me with you," she asks.

"No." Blade steps toward her. She throws her arms up to shield herself, and I grab his arm.

"She was the only one who showed me kindness. Please, if she wants to come, let her. She protected me from Gia. She fed me and brought me clothes."

"No."

"Please! We can't leave her here, anyway. She could sound an alarm and get us caught. She has to come with us."

I remember Emma's words that someday she would get away from here. She was kind to me, and Tiernan has hurt her, too. If I have a chance to help her, I want to. I am also a little afraid of what Tiernan will do to her if he finds I had escaped on her watch.

I place my hand on Blade's chest. "Please," I say again.

He growls his frustration. "All the goddesses," Blade swears. "Fine. Let's go." He points a finger at Emma. "You hold your own, or you're on your own."

He drags me behind him as he runs. His men cause distractions, drawing the attention of the night watch, allowing us to go unseen. We make it out of the compound and stop for a moment. I bend over, my hands on my knees. Blade scans the area. I am breathing heavily, and sweat streams between my breasts. It finally hits me: I'm being rescued.

He leaves me no time to catch my breath. He grabs my hand, and we hit the ground at a dead run toward the waterline. His long strides make it impossible for me to keep up. He loses patience and scoops me up into his enormous arms. Behind me, I hear Emma struggling to keep up.

When we reach the boat, he sets me on my feet. His eyes scan the surrounding area again, always looking. We scramble in as quickly as we can. The water I used to find happiness in is now an icy, frigid chill.

One man is pushing the boat offshore when Emma finally catches up and runs into the water. She throws herself over the side of the boat and rolls onto the sole. She hits with a thud, and air whooshes out of her. I try to help her when I catch a scent--a scent I know all too well.

"Stop!" I cry out.

All movement ceases. I arch my neck, throw my head up, and sniff. I rear back and howl, the guttural sound reverberating in my throat.

Confused but not bothered, Blade gestures to his warrior to push off.

In seconds, out of the line of trees to the right, Willow and her mate are running for us at full speed. Each mouth holds a pup, and around Willow's neck is the amulet.

The wolves leap into the boat with us. Emma squeals, but she stops when I kneel and wrap my arms around Willow's neck to hug her tightly.

Blade takes control of the situation, unruffled by the events. He barks a few orders, and in seconds, we are at sea. Several large males work to propel the boat forward. I wonder why they didn't have a power-boat, then realize it was probably because of the noise.

For a good long while, Blade mumbles about crazy females and wild wolves. Despite the situation, I can't help being amused. I have to bite the inside of my cheek, so I don't laugh out loud--and then shame washes over me that I can even laugh.

Weak and dog-tired, I lean against Willow, her pups curled next to me. For the first time in what feels like years rather than days, I feel no fear. Under the twinkling of the stars, I fall asleep.

❧

The journey is long. Exhaustion plagues me, but I wake to Emma's cackle. I can't return to sleep. She flirts shamelessly with the males, who mostly ignore her.

Everyone on the boat has been kind to me, except Blade. He isn't unkind, just stiff and formal. I try to engage him in conversation, but he merely grunts at me. I notice that when he isn't busy scanning our surroundings, his eyes are on me. He is always on guard and ready to fight, his right hand resting near a weapon.

Willow and the pups stay close to me, but her mate sits at Blade's feet. Emma annoys him with her rambling. I sense he doesn't like her, and when he looks at her, it's clear he would rather throw her overboard than listen to her.

Apprehension sets in as I think of everything that occurred in the last few days. Was my birthday only a couple of days ago? I stop myself. I will think about everything later. I don't know where we are going, but I know it can't be worse than what I just escaped.

I look up at the night sky, thinking of my foster father. I pray to the goddesses for him and for my birth father. Then I thank them for my rescue, for Willow, and for maybe having my first real friend in Emma.

In the distance, I see little specks of golden light that bob in a sea of darkness—the shadows of bodies in the rays. The stars and the moon overhead illuminate the cliffs like a mystical realm. I ask Blade if that is where we are going.

"Yes. That's Moonstone Island, the home of your pack."

I clasp my hands together in front of my waist, and that's when I notice I still have on Tiernan's betrothal ring. I am wearing the sign of Red Blood. Blade looks at my hands and sees the ring. He gently takes my hand in his and pulls the ring from my finger. He rolls it between his fingers, and then he sees the sign of Red Blood. "Tiernan?" he asks.

Embarrassed, I still won't lie. "Yes."

He draws his arm back and tosses the ring into the ocean. He whips it so far--I don't even hear it plop into the water.

"Care to explain that?" he asks.

"Not really," I reply.

"Well, someone is going to." He looks at Emma.

If she starts telling it, we will still be listening come daybreak. Plus, she doesn't know everything. "I'll tell you," I concede. I feel heat rush to my face, shame in my voice.

I tell him about meeting Tiernan when I was fifteen and about our relationship. I tell him about Tiernan's promises and our few arguments. When I get to the part about Tiernan's proposal and how I found my foster father, a dark hissing sound comes from deep within Blade's throat. I force myself to continue. I tell Blade what happened when I went to Tiernan for help. At this point, everyone is listening with rapt attention. Blade's eyes glow yellow, fury blackening the air surrounding him.

"Did you give yourself to him?" he asks quietly.

"I did not--almost, but no."

He lets out a huge breath. "I will make sure he never gets near you. If he tries, I will kill him. I will rip out his still-beating heart and hand it to you."

I shiver at the anger in his voice, but Emma snorts loudly. Blade's eyes nearly close. I can see just a gleam of yellow through the narrow slits. Anger and rage reverberate from him, but before he says anything, one male whispers something to Emma. She gasps, then looks at Blade, her eyes wide. She looks at him with respect and maybe a bit of fear. I wonder what that was about but decide it isn't time to ask.

I look up at the night sky, the moon covered by the hazy clouds that throw rays that reflect off the water. "Father, what do I do now? I can't believe you left me. I have no one except Willow. I belong to no pack. I have no family. I am truly… alone," I whisper.

I swallow the tears that fight to escape, holding back sobs that settle deep in the pit of my stomach.

# CHAPTER 9

*"Friendship is certainly the finest balm for the pangs of disappointed love." -
Jane Austen, Northanger Abbey*

When we get close to land, males run out and pull the boat to shore. Everyone gets off and moves to the side except me.

As relieved as I am to have escaped my death sentence, I can't help but be afraid. I don't know this place, these shifters. I need to have blind faith that they will help me, protect me--and I no longer trust my own judgment, not on anything. What if what I am walking into is as bad as what I just got rescued from?

The knot in my throat tightens as Blade grabs me around the waist and lifts me out of the boat. Uncomfortable at his touch, I quickly step to the side. The crowd parts, their lanterns held high.

I look at Blade and see him clearly for the first time. He has tattooed biceps and wears bars through the cartilage of his ears. His wheat-streaked brown hair is pulled back in a man-bun. He has a scar that runs diagonally through his left eyebrow. There must be a story behind that, I think. Shifters heal quickly from basic injuries, and rarely is there any sign left. I'll have to remember to ask.

His skin is darker than mine, a beautiful golden hue. As attractive as he is, his size and build are overwhelming. He is massive. He has a tough look to him, dressed as a warrior with his weapons within easy reach.

It hits me like blunt force trauma: Blade's a gamma. My rescuer is third in command and head warrior. He is both feared and respected. He can sense danger before the rest of the pack, and he will act on it quickly and efficiently. This is his role. This is his calling. He has the best battle skills and fears nothing. Gammas are known to look death in the eye and challenge it.

Murmurs from the crowd draw my attention from Blade. Two males walk down the path, side by side. A third male is off the right shoulder of the older male. When they reach me, the older one speaks.

"My dear, it is our honor to have you among us. We have never given up hope that you would return." He takes my hands in his, and I feel immensely uncomfortable. "I am Malachi Lycidas, the pack master and alpha since your father's death. My son, Killian," he gestures to the younger male next to him. Killian bows slightly. "This is Lorcan Hemming, head of our pack council." Lorcan steps forward and bows as well. Why are they bowing to me?

I introduce myself. "Amirah Foalan. This is my friend, Emma." Emma acknowledges the introduction with a curtsey as if she is greeting royalty. I roll my eyes.

Malachi looks at Willow, the amulet still around her neck like a collar.

"That's my Willow. She is my guard. She stays with me."

"Yes, well, you won't need her to stay with you. I've assigned Blade to your safety, and I assure you, *safe* you will be. Uh, Willow has a friend?" he asks, looking at the large male wolf standing at Blade's feet.

"Her mate. He stays with me, too; so do the pups."

"Yes, my dear, as you wish, but it is unnecessary. Blade would give his life to protect yours--but whatever will make you feel safe. I promise you, no harm will come to you. You are the Chosen."

He bends over in front of Willow, reaching his hand out so she can sniff him. When she accepts him, he looks at me and says, "May I?" I nod. He removes the amulet from Willow's neck and hands it to his son.

"Killian, do the honors."

Killian bows again then attaches the amulet around my neck. Blue light flows out of the amulet. The members of the pack that line the path dropped to a knee.

The alpha turns to the crowd, his back to me. I'm tense, and I don't know why. Blade places his hand on my lower back. I feel safe with him near, but I don't like when he touches me. There's no anger or malice in his touch; I think I'm just scared. Too much has happened in too short of a time. I am unable to process it, unable to accept it.

"Dark Moon Pack, she is here: the Chosen!" Malachi announces with great fanfare.

Malachi and his son flank me, one on each side. Blade and Lorcan stand behind us. They escort me down the path, and as we pass each shifter, they bow their heads. I look behind me for Emma, relieved to see she is still there.

When we reach the door of the gothic mansion, Lorcan steps in front of me. "Amirah, we have laid your foster father to rest on our grounds. I wanted you to know that we honored him."

Tears flood my eyes; grief makes my chest tighten. "Thank you," I say. I appreciate the thoughtfulness. He deserves more--he deserves so much more--but at least he isn't rotting alone in the cabin.

Once inside the mansion, Malachi addresses me. "We will take leave and let you rest. Tomorrow is soon enough to tend to business. Blade will escort you to your rooms."

"Thank you."

Blade takes my arm, escorting me through a corridor and down a long hall. The cold, gray, stone walls that curve over the walkway give the passage a sense of mystery--a mystery of what may hide in the shadows of the hand-built columns. The ancient floors, dimly lit by lanterns, have felt many footsteps over the centuries. I imagine whispers from the souls of the past.

"It's fine, Amirah. There is nothing to fear. This is where you belong. I trained to be your protector my entire life. You are safe."

He opens the door to a room and allows me to enter first. It is dimly lit with a gigantic bed against the back wall, sconces hanging on both sides. Large, comfortable pillows are piled high, and a fluffy blanket covers the mattress. A wood and steel chandelier hangs down from the center of the ceiling and casts light around the room. There is a sizable stone fireplace, wiped clean of ash and laid with fresh wood. The room has a slick marble floor that is sure to radiate a chill in the room. Regardless of its lack of modern style, it is breathtakingly beautiful.

Blade lights the fire, and heat begins to fill the room.

"Will you guard all night?" I ask.

"Amirah, I will stay outside your door until you settle, then I will retire to my rooms. I will be outside your door before you awaken in the morning. Where you go, I will go--unless you dismiss me. Until you feel safe, and until we ensure there is no retaliation from Red Blood, I will be your shadow."

At the door, he turns back to me.

"They have provided clothes for you, and when you are ready for bed," he jiggles the doorknob, "there's a lock. Use it. Someone will bring food soon."

"Thank you, Blade. For the rescue, but for the other stuff, too--for listening, for not judging me…."

"Rest. You are safe now. Probably safer than you've been your entire life." He leaves, Willow's mate following him. How interesting, I think.

Moments later, Emma bursts through the door like a hurricane, and a flurry of words flies out of her mouth in a rush.

"*Mmm*, girl, the males 'round here are yummy. Which one is the one ya want?" she asks.

I just look at her. Is she nuts? I am pretty sure she is, to be honest. "None. I want no males. I'll not give my heart to another to be shattered. I'll not trust again just to be deceived."

"Ya ain't gotta give em yer heart, but ya can have a grand time, otherwise," she says.

"I can't give my body and not give my heart; they go hand in hand. And since I will never again have faith in my own judgment or believe in another in that way, I will remain alone."

"Right, well, we will work on that," Emma says, and as quickly as she had come into the room, she leaves.

I wash and eat, then change into a delicate nightgown I find in the armoire. The lace and silk wash over my skin with a delicacy I have never known. I check the locks on the door and the window then climb into bed. I settle into the softness of the feather pillows.

Did I lock the door, though? I get up to double-check. Will I ever feel safe again?

I flip from side to side, looking at the door and the window. Thoughts of the past forty-eight hours overwhelm me until exhaustion takes me into a restless sleep.

# CHAPTER 10

*"Hold to the now, the here, through which all future plunges to the past." -*
*James Joyce*

The next morning, I wake to sunlight shining through the windows. I dress quickly and open the door. Blade is there, just as he said he would be.

"Are you ready to break your fast?" he asks. He has such an odd way with words sometimes.

"Yes."

He escorts me to a large dining room where buffets of food line the wall. Killian is at the table eating, and he looks up when we enter. Blade moves to the side of the door, always on guard. I make a plate for myself and sit down at the table. Malachi soon follows, grabs a plate for himself, and sits down.

"Good morning, dear. You look rested. We have much to do today. Preparation has begun for the ceremony and celebration."

Killian snorts, then clears his throat. He looks at me with contempt. While I sense I have nothing to fear from him, I also sense he doesn't like me. His father narrows his eyes at him, and he quickly returns to his meal. I look at Blade, who is observing the exchange with interest.

Emma comes and fills the silence with excited chatter. It is too early to deal with her, but since I brought her, I have no choice. Her mouth never stops moving, and I wonder if she even talks in her sleep. She bats her eyelashes at Killian, addressing him before me. He appears amused at her flirtations but not interested.

She must have been too much for the alpha, I think, because he soon excuses himself, taking sweet rolls and his mug with him.

"Aren't ya excited? I bet yer *so* excited. All this fuss just fer ya. I hope I get to help ya get ready. They said after is filled with drinkin' 'n dancin' 'n games." She took a quick breath and continued. "Do ya think I can at least peek at the ballroom?" she asks.

Fully expecting her to continue rambling, I don't respond. I also don't know what she is talking about. Malachi referenced a ceremony, but for what?

"Over the top, in my opinion," Killian mutters, "all this fuss."

A servant comes to get Emma to begin her training, and she leaves as noisily as she arrived. An agitated Killian and I sit at the table in silence. Blade stays on guard at the door, never relaxed. I almost wish Emma was still here, chattering like a magpie--*almost*.

"What's the celebration for?" I ask Killian, breaking the silence.

Killian jerks his head up and looks at me. "The ceremony is for you. It's for you to take your crown as the Chosen, a celebration after for the entire pack."

"Seriously?"

"Yes, seriously--though it's stupid if you ask me."

"Well, I didn't ask."

"Right. Yeah, well, I am to be your escort and guide you through the process, though I don't see why you need an escort."

"Praise Morrigan, and aren't I lucky to have you as an escort? I'd rather not have one." I sit back in the chair and fold my arms across my chest.

Ignoring my comment, Killian continues. "The ceremony is at the cove on the north side of the island. We walk through the pack, much like last night. My father and Lorcan will be at the end of the walk. The seer speaks, the crown goes on your head, you accept your role, and then we come back here where the mansion is open on the main floor for all to come and celebrate."

"I don't think I need an escort for that if you'd rather not. I assure you I can walk unattended."

"I couldn't get out of it if I tried." He gets up from the table and leaves. I look at Blade, who is scowling at Killian's back, a deep frown firmly in place.

Blade escorts me to the council hall, where they tell me more details about the ceremony. Malachi introduces me to the council, which is very formal and makes me feel like a bug being watched under a microscope. Afterward, Blade escorts me back to my room. I try to read from a leather-bound book I pluck off the shelf. I can't concentrate. I pace the room for what feels like hours.

"Come on, Willow." I pick up her pups, and we leave the room. At the end of the hall stands Blade, Willow's mate, by his side. He is talking to a younger male who I had seen with him before.

"I thought I'd bring Willow to see..." I gestured at her mate.

"Warlock. I call him Warlock."

"Warlock," I repeat.

He shrugs. "I figured I had to call him something since he won't leave me."

He turns and addresses the younger male. "Keep training, Caleb; we will address this later on." The young male bows slightly in deference to Blade's position then leaves.

"Can we take the wolves for a walk?" I ask, wanting an excuse for fresh air and to look around.

"Amirah, you are not a captive here. If you want to do something, you do it. You are free to do as you please. Do you wish me to accompany you on the walk?"

"Yes. Yes, I do."

Blade, the wolves, and I walk outside for hours. He explains to me the lay of the island, how the pack works. We carry the pups, and Willow and Warlock play, rolling on the ground. He really *is* nice. He shows a judgment-free kindness to me, though I am humiliated that he knows how foolish I was with Tiernan. When we return to the mansion, I ask him if we can walk again the next day, and he agrees.

The next day, while the pack prepares for the ceremony, Blade and I walk in the morning and evening. I confide in him about my guilt for my foster father's death and my shame in myself for falling for Tiernan. Blade has a fierce hatred for Tiernan that seems to grow every day. Anger radiates off him like the blast from an inferno. His eyes glow yellow at the mere mention of Tiernan's name.

Blade became my friend after just a few conversations. I know I am safe with him. No longer haunted by lies and secrets, I am truly free.

The morning of the ceremony, I am up early. Still tired from a restless sleep, worry cloaks me in fear of the unknown. As she who is Chosen, what will my duties be? When I asked, they said I'll know. How will I know? They said it is my destiny. A heaviness shrouds my small frame, and it feels like a rock is sitting in the pit of my stomach.

At my request, Emma comes to help me get ready. I need Emma's relentless chatter to distract my worried mind. After I eat a breakfast of sweetbreads and fruit, I bathe in rosewater; the scent sticks to my skin and hair and reminds me of a garden.

Emma helps me into the gown provided for me. The green is as deep as an emerald, with soft peach threading along the borders. The bodice has the same soft peach in an ornate design. The embroidered Dark Moon symbol sits between my breasts. The arms are a straight sleeve that flares delicately at my wrist that is adorned with cream edging. The gown drapes elegantly and widens at my cream-colored booted ankles. It is of the softest silk and slides along my skin like a glove.

"Emma?"

"Hmm?" She runs the brush through my long black hair, then coils and pins it against my head. Curls rest softly against my cheek. She gives the top of my hair volume so the crown will frame my face when it lays on my forehead.

"I don't know that I want to do this."

With her tongue between her teeth, she concentrates on her task. "I don't think ya have much of a choice." She moves in front of me and pats my hand. "So much has changed for ya in a short time. You grieve--not just for yer pa, yer home, but also you grieve Tiernan."

"I don't care about him," I protest.

"You do, if'n fer no other than the love ya thought ya had 'n who ya thought he was. He was nev'r what he made ya b'lieve. He is a savage.

Ya have somethin' here--a normal life, even if there are responsibilities. Let the past go. Grab yer future, and fer once, be happy."

She stands up and plays with one of my curls, shaping it with her fingers. She grabs my chin in her hands and looks at me closely.

"Ya do have a choice, but do ya, really? This is yer destiny. That's what they say." She goes back to fixing my hair. For once, her chattering stops, and she concentrates on the styling.

She finishes, and I stand in front of an ornate floor-length mirror. I touch my silky hair gently, afraid to mess it up. I run my hands down the sides of the glamorous gown; the cold silk soothes my fingers. I meet Emma's eyes in the mirror, and she smiles widely at me. There is a knock on the door. "Come in," I say.

Blade enters. "It's time, Amirah."

Emma takes my hand again. "Be happy. This be a good thing,"

I don't respond to Emma's optimism, but I can't help but wonder, is it really a good thing? If it was so good, why wasn't I here all along?

# CHAPTER 11

*"Friendship... is born at the moment when one man says to another 'What! You too? I thought that no one but myself...'" -C.S. Lewis, The Four Loves*

At the door, Killian stands tall, his eyes on mine. How handsome he looks in his pants and embroidered tunic. His hair is a mixture of brown and dark blonde. His eyes are as green as my sparkling gown. His face is unshaven, scruffy, and immensely attractive.

Killian and Blade, side by side, are a beautiful sight to behold--so beautiful that Emma sighs, her admiration clear in the soft sound. They are opposites in so many ways: Blade, tough, strong, and imposing; Killian, a massive shifter, yes, but nowhere as massive as Blade. He is regal in appearance, his confidence absolute. They take my breath away.

Killian and Blade both stare at me, and Blade's jaw drops. This is the only time they've seen me not in my pants and tunics. Time stands still like a broken grandfather clock.

Emma cackles then clears her throat. "Git on with it then, or you'll be late." Her voice snaps us out of our thoughts. Killian offers me his arm, and I lay my palm gently on the crook.

"Let's get this shit over with. I have plans for later," Killian says.

"Well, I wouldn't want to interfere with your plans, so let's go." The mood is no longer as serene as it was just moments before.

His head jerks as Blade raps him upside it, as male friends do. "Asshole," Blade mutters under his breath.

The walk to the site is long, and I grow tired of Killian's grouchy comments and muttered complaints. Blade, my ever-present protector, tries his best to talk over Killian's snide comments. He, too, is dressed for the occasion. He has traded his battle clothes for a tunic and pants with the pack symbols embroidered throughout the sleeves. The shoulders are decorated with the pins of the gamma. His hair is untied, and wisps of it blow in the wind.

It seems like we are walking forever when we reach the cove of the coastal inlet. A young girl with green eyes and long blond hair greets us. She is our escort and will start the ceremony. She has pale, freckled skin and wears a rose-colored gown that compliments her skin color. She drops to one knee as we step through the keyhole and onto the ceremonial grounds. A bouquet made of beach morning glories, wood asters, and violets rest in her arms.

"For you, a gift to honor the Chosen." She rises and hands me the bouquet.

"Thank you." I cradle the array of flora in my left arm. That simply, the ceremony begins.

She moves behind me to straighten my gown, then takes position next to Blade.

Killian looks at me. "You ready for this?"

"I guess."

"Well, don't let us force you; you can turn around and head back to Tiernan."

Blade growls deep in his throat. The ground shakes violently beneath our feet, and a small slide of rocks rolls down the hill to our left. Killian looks back at him.

"What's your problem, Blade?" he asks.

"Never say that again. You go too far."

Unconcerned, Killian turns away. Blade's anger still reverberates. It pleases me to know he is so protective of me that the mere mention of Tiernan causes a miniature rockslide.

For the first time, I look at the thousands of shifters who stand in their finery. My heart thuds as the pink and orange rays of the setting sun glint off the warriors' swords and armor. They look at me with hope, and I know deep in my heart what an honor it is to be here with the Dark Moon pack. I will do what they need me to do as Chosen.

Killian escorts me down the path. The shifters bow or take a knee as we come upon them. We reach the end where Malachi, Lorcan, and the seer, Serenity, stand clothed in their finest beside the ceremonial altar. On the altar, the crown rests on a red felt pillow; its gemstones twinkle like hundreds of winking lights. Flowers and sea glass of every color surround it. I feel everyone's eyes on me.

The seer steps forward. "Dark Moon pack of Moonstone Island," she says, raising her arms high. Cheers echo behind me.

"Before you is the Chosen. The guardian of all children. The protector of the elders. The champion and keeper of The Faoladh, from which all of our pack and many more have descended."

The deep blue of the ocean on our right blends into the bright pink and red of the setting sun. Rays of blue light surround the altar. The glitter dust shines bright, and magic and excitement spark the air.

She faces me, "This night, I ask as the sun sets, for all to see: will you accept your fate as Chosen and fulfill your destiny? By order of the goddesses, when you accept your fate, will you devote your life as the Ruler of Faoladh, to all our kind? Your rule to protect the sanctity of all?"

I freeze. My heart stops beating, and my brain stops working. Killian elbows me.

"Answer." He rolls his eyes.

"I will," I say, and cheers explode from the crowd.

"Will you take your rightful position in the Dark Moon pack and sit at the side of the alpha? Will you devote yourself to the wellbeing of the Dark Moon pack, your guardians, your protectors, who offer all that you need?"

I needed no prompt this time. "I will."

The shifters scream and clap, and whistles pierce the air.

Lorcan steps forward and clasps a bracelet on my wrist. The part human, part wolf symbol of the Faoladh is engraved on the band. The representation of a clan of shifters that causes no harm, lives in peace and kindness, and holds true the traditions of long ago. It sparkles in the light, beautiful in its simplicity.

The seer steps forward and places a pin on my shoulder with the Dark Moon insignia engraved in its oval center: the full moon with clouds shadowing its beam of light. I look at the pin on my shoulder, and my heart fills.

Malachi steps forward, the crown in his hands. Silence takes over the crowd. The only sound is the howling of the ocean and the song of the crashing waves. He places the crown on my head, the band sitting in an ornamental 'v' in the center of my forehead. The gems and symbols adorning the band shine bright. "Your fathers would be so proud of you," he says. He kisses me on my left cheek, then my right, and steps away.

The pulsing heartbeat of a drum sounds. At first, it is soft, and then it grows in speed and volume. A spiritual and physical contentment surrounds us all. The drum gets louder until I feel the pulse beneath my feet. My heartbeat matches the rhythmic tempo. Blue rays of light flash through the air like tiny bolts of lightning. The drums slow in tempo and volume until the sound disappears.

Killian turns us to the crowd. Some females shed tears, the young hop around in excitement, and the males stand with reverence and admiration in their eyes.

Killian escorts me back down the path. Flowers of various colors litter the path before us, their sweet scent perfuming the air. I feel in my heart that this is where I should be and what I am supposed to do. I hope with every part of me that my fathers are proud.

Halfway down the path, there is a *'thwish'* like the sound of an arrow string being released, followed by a *'whoosh'* as an arrow flies, heading straight for me. I freeze in shock. Blade pushes me out of the way, and Killian knocks me to the ground and covers me with his body. Footsteps thud, screams echo around me, but I can see nothing.

Killian jumps off me, and he and Blade shift. Their immense size and speed are captivating. They take off after a hooded man trying to escape through the narrow passages in the cliffs, their regalia in tattered piles at my feet.

I sit there, shocked. The gentle hands of Lorcan lift me back on my feet. He dusts the dirt off my gown, then licks his finger and wipes a smudge on my cheek.

"There, now--as beautiful as ever. Are you okay?"

"I'm fine. What happened?"

He picks up the arrow. I pale at how close it is to where I was on the ground. That arrow was meant for me.

"This was meant for you. Come, let's return to the mansion and await word from Blade."

Warriors surround Lorcan and me as he escorts me back to the mansion. My legs are like jelly, and my hands shake the entire way.

He places me in the sitting room with Caleb on guard. It upsets me that there was an attempt on my life, and I worry about Blade and Killian. When the door opens, Willow and Warlock enter to lie at my feet, and I start to calm. As upset and as scared as I am, I am still safe. No harm would come to me here, they had said to me. Now, I believe it.

Emma comes in and helps me tidy my hair and clothes, and the young girl who gave me the bouquet earlier comes in with tea and cakes. Emma asks her if she has heard anything.

"Caleb told me before you arrived that Blade and Killian captured the hooded male and are questioning him in the cells. He said that Killian had to pull Blade off the male before he ripped his throat out. Killian said that they needed information, not blood. That's all I know."

A shiver runs through me when I envision the wrath of Blade, but I can't help but notice that when the girl said Caleb's name, there was a twinkle in her eye and a soft smile gracing her lips.

"What's your name?" I ask her.

"Brionough." She curtsies. "You can call me Bria, and I am your female in waiting, your companion and assistant. I am pleased to have been chosen."

"It's nice to officially meet you. There's no need for you to sit in here as we wait for news," I said, giving her leave.

Emma and I sit and wait in silence. My knees jiggle, and I twist the bracelet on my wrist. My nerves are overwhelming me.

Several hours of silence later, Blade, Killian, Lorcan, and Malachi enter. Caleb still stands guard at the door.

"Did you get him?" I asked, standing up from my chair. I'm afraid that Tiernan or Eamon somehow found me.

"We did," Blade responds simply.

"And?"

"And *what*, princess?" Killian says. "Someone let an arrow loose at you. We caught him. That's all you need to know."

"That is not all I need to know--and do *not* call me princess." I stomped over to him. We glare at each other, toe-to-toe and nose-to=nose, nostrils flaring in anger. I have *really* had enough of his attitude. It was *my* life that was threatened, not his.

Lorcan steps between us, and Malachi lectures Killian in a hushed voice.

It is Blade who gives me an honest answer.

"We caught him, and we questioned him. He said he was paid in food to take the shot at you. He is poor and has a family to feed, so he took the offer. He doesn't know who it was who called the hit; it was arranged by note. He will remain our prisoner," he says as casually as if he were discussing what he ate for dinner.

"And his family?"

"I will give his mate a position on the outside, enough to provide for the family," Malachi answers. "The celebration continues as planned, but Blade and his warriors will check everyone for weapons. Lorcan and Killian will stay with you, now."

"Just how I wanted to spend the entire evening: babysitting the princess," Killian says.

On his way out the door, Blade calls him an asshole. Again.

Lorcan merely tells Killian to shut up.

Who the hell does he think he is? I'll be damned if he is going to babysit me or call me a princess. I stand up tall and tilt my chin up to show my strength and a confidence I don't fully feel. I address Killian with a voice pulled from the depths within me. I know that it's now or never to let Killian know I am no longer taking his swiping and nasty comments.

"I am not a princess, Killian. I am the Chosen, and you better start treating me with the respect the position deserves."

I whirl to the door, not giving him a chance to respond. My head still high, my anger apparent, I slam the door with the force of a gull wind. The crack of wood against wood echoes down the hallowed halls. Yes, he needed to be reminded, even if I'm not sure what all that exactly means.

# CHAPTER 12

*"I will not say: do not weep; for not all tears are an evil." -J.R.R. Tolkien, The Return of the King*

They escort me to the celebration. It is becoming a lively event. Food is plentiful, set as a buffet so that anyone that wishes can serve themselves. Beautiful arrangements of flowers that match my bouquet sit on tables and stands. Their sweet perfume mingles with the mouthwatering scents of the culinary delights. The musicians in the ballroom play lively music, and the shifters dance and frolic in fun. Younger males and females flirt and talk. Elders are grouped together with their mates close by.

Killian's duty requires him to dance with me. With great pleasure, I step on his toes, muttering a '*whoops*' or a '*sorry*' each time. He complains that I can't dance and that I lack grace. I step on his toes harder.

The entertainers in the courtyard are amusing, and happiness from everyone abounds. The threat from earlier today seems to be forgotten as everyone celebrates.

The alpha checks on me regularly but has many things to attend to. Blade is on duty, so I am supposed to stay with Killian. I'd rather be left with a python, if I'm being honest. Thankfully, after our dance, he stays busy flirting shamelessly with a brown-haired female. Lorcan takes pity and sits down next to me. He's so very kind and always a gentleman. He lacks Blade's violent edge, as well as Killian's attitude, and for that, I am thankful. It is easy for us to just be in the moment.

After a few minutes, he asks me to dance. I can see the hesitation in his eyes as he looks at his own toes.

"Of course," I answer.

Moments later, my hand is in his, his other hand is on my waist, and he chuckles in my ear. "You stepped on his toes on purpose. You dance beautifully."

"Maybe--or maybe not. Perhaps you are an exquisite partner."

He lifts his head back and laughs. We continue to dance, one dance after the other.

As we dance, the hair on the back of my neck prickles, and I feel someone looking at me. Uneasy after what happened earlier, I scan the room to see Killian's glare from across the ballroom. His lip is lifted in a snarl, anger in his eyes.

"You don't remember me, do you?" Lorcan asks and brings my attention back to him.

The questions startles me, and I look at him closely.

"I'm sorry, but I don't."

"We were together a lot before," he says. "Our fathers were close, almost like brothers."

"I don't remember much from when I was little." I feel bad, but I don't have many memories from before the cabin, and I have none of Lorcan.

He nods sadly. "I understand. We were once good friends."

The dancing ends, and he escorts me to a chair, where we sit in silence for some time and watch the revelers. My eyes sweep across the room as I look for Blade until I find him talking to a group of warriors. Within seconds, his gaze settles on me. He smiles at me, and I smile back with a little wave.

Lorcan clears his throat. I ask him a question that has been weighing on me.

"Do you know where my father is?" I ask.

He nods. "Your father and your foster father are placed in our sacred grounds, near to my own father."

I feel like I need to say goodbye--to both of them. "Will you take me? Now?" I ask, afraid that he will say no and that I won't have the courage to ask again.

Lorcan calls Blade over and whispers in his ear. Blade frowns but nods and hands him his own short dagger that sits at his lower back. Then Blade goes back to his post.

Lorcan stands and checks his sword in its sheath, attaches the dagger, then holds his hand out to me. "Come, we will go now. It's a bit of a walk."

While we walk to the burial grounds, he fills the silence with stories about our fathers and even my foster father. He makes me laugh at some of the things we got into when we were little. A pair we were, often getting into mischief.

He remembers my mother. If I have few memories of my birth father, I have even fewer of her. I want to ask him what happened to her, but we arrive at the gravesite before I have the chance.

Tall gothic fences surround the grounds. A large tree sits in the center with a stone bench underneath. We push through the gate, and suddenly, I am overwhelmed with sadness--not just mine, but of the many others who have passed through the gates.

Lorcan leads me to my fathers' headstones. Both are intricately carved, their names and the years of their births and deaths engraved into marble plaques. I run my fingertips on each of the plaques, tears filling my eyes.

"I wish I could leave you to say what you need without me over your shoulder, but I cannot. I promised Blade I would not leave you for even a second. So, you're stuck with me. I won't intrude; take your time."

Feeling a fondness for this male with whom I once had a close friendship, I look at him closely. I wish I remembered. How conservative he is, his green-gold eyes always so intense. He never has a hair out of place. It must be something he has grown into, given the stories he told me of our times past.

"There are worse males I could be stuck with--like Killian," I say to ease his concern at not giving me proper privacy.

He laughs, then steps a foot away--close enough to stand watch and get to me quickly, far enough to give me the privacy he thinks I should have.

I say a prayer to the goddesses for my fathers. Silvery slivers of tears slide down my face in the moonlight as I stand there, lost in my memories.

Lorcan comes over, wraps his arm around me, and pulls my face into his chest. He kisses the top of my head and offers words of condolence and sympathy. His kindness makes me cry harder. My shoulders wrack with uncontrollable sobs. He sits down on the ground, pulls me onto his lap, and lets me cry. My grief is overwhelming; I don't know if I will ever stop crying. The tears keep flowing, and he keeps wiping them away.

I don't know how long we sit there on the cold ground surrounded by the spirits of loved ones lost. He says nothing and lets me cry until I have no tears left to shed. "I'm sorry," I sniffle.

"Amirah, you don't need to apologize for grieving. Your loss has been huge. They forced you into isolation, sheltered out of necessity. You had a closeness with your foster father because he was all you had. Your birth father--his love for you was as fierce as any alpha's. You may not remember, but your heart knows. You need to grieve so that you can heal."

He hands me a lace embroidered handkerchief. I dry my eyes and wipe my nose.

"Thank you."

"You're welcome," he replies and pulls me to my feet.

"Not for the hanky--well, yes, that, but thank you for being my friend when I was little, for sharing my father with me, and for being my friend now." I stand on tiptoe and kiss his cheek in friendly appreciation.

He clasps my hand to his chest. "I will always be your friend, Amirah. Always."

He escorts me back to the mansion.

In the doorway to the ballroom, Blade is still standing on duty. Lorcan's hand is still on my elbow when we enter. I feel Killian's glare. When I find him amongst the revelers, he frowns at me. As much as it pleases me to see the pack have such a grand time, I think it's time for me to leave.

"Lorcan, do I have to stay until this is over? It's just… it looks like it could go on for hours, and my head hurts. I know this celebration is for me, but I need to lie down."

"Give me a minute, and then I'll make your excuses." He walks over to Blade, says something to him that makes him scan the floor until his eyes land on me. He cocks his head to the side and takes in my red eyes and tear-streaked makeup. He nods once, motions to another warrior, then makes his way across the floor to me.

"You wish to retire, Amirah?"

"Yes, please."

"Are you okay?"

"Fine. It's just--it's a lot. Everything is just… a *lot*."

He nods slowly. "Okay, let's go."

He escorts me to my room, not asking questions or berating me for leaving. As usual, there's no judgment. At the door, he grabs the knob and opens it. Before I can enter, he grabs my arm, sympathy in his eyes.

"Amirah, I know you have been through a lot. I know your pain is raw, your fear is real, and your heart is hurting--but tomorrow is another day. Thousands of shifters all over the world are counting on you to do what you promised to do. I'll help you, but you're gonna have to step up."

"I know. I will. Just give me tonight, Blade. Give me tonight to mourn my fathers, mourn the loss of my heart to someone who didn't deserve it, and tomorrow, I will be grateful for all that I now have and step into my rule, whatever that may be. Please, just give me tonight." I look straight at him, so he knows I mean what I am saying.

He softly brushes his thumb across my chin, one slow stroke. "Good-night, Amirah. Sleep well."

"Wait."

He raises his eyebrow, the scar through the center puckering at the movement.

"Do you need something, Amirah?"

"No, I just… can you stay for a little while? I feel safer when you are near."

Blade smiles at me. "Of course. You settle in, and I'll come back with some cocoa. I assure you, Amirah, you are now and always will be safe when I am near. I have committed my life to keeping yours safe."

Blade returns, and we sit in front of the blazing fire. He entertains me with tales of his training when he was younger and the many battles he has won with such enthusiasm that I can't stop the smile that graces my lips. I fall asleep to the comfort of his deep voice.

*"Each friend represents a world in us, a world possibly not born until they arrive, and it is only by this meeting that a new world is born." -Anais Nin*

A week after the ceremony, I stretch my arms above my head and soak up the rays of sunlight that shine through my bedroom window. My brain is overloaded with information from the past week, and I'm tired.

Lorcan, Blade, and Killian have the job of educating me in the ways of the Chosen. Lorcan is kind and generous with his praise. Blade is tough and demanding when he teaches me the battle history of our pack. Killian works with me on ceremonies and rituals. What was once the hardest time spent learning becomes fun when Killians' resentment toward me ceases. I still enjoy our verbal spars and matching wit against wit. I rejoice at no longer being haunted by the secrets or lies that kept me awake at night in the past. I feel completely safe. There haven't been additional attempts on my life, and if there are any to come, Blade will handle them, surely.

After breakfast, I head to the library to meet with Lorcan. He is already waiting for me, as usual. The walls are filled with rows of leather-bound books that lend the air a musty smell.

Today's focus is on the differences between the Faoladh, from which my pack descends, and the Teutonic line from Gilgamesh, which is where Red Blood comes from. The Faoladh are wolf shifters who live their life by a code. We are protectors. We are peaceful unless we need to be otherwise. We praise the Celtic goddesses and honor their goodness. The Teutonic are evil--pure evil. Tiernan and his pack of heathens fit with them fabulously.

It's not long before I grow weary of hearing about the Blood Thirst. Lorcan sees that I don't want to hear anymore and suggests we walk in the garden.

With my arm in his, we stroll along the brick path. Aromatic flowers surround us.

"Let's sit," Lorcan says.

He gestures toward the bench near a fountain that has long since dried. I sit, and he lounges next to me with his arm slung along the back of the seat. He tells me more stories of our childhood. I love hearing them, and I know that our friendship was true and is now firmly rooted in both history and the present. I wish so much that I could remember. I lift my head toward the sun and let the rays warm me.

"Amirah," Lorcan says.

"Hmm?"

"Can we talk for a minute?"

I laugh softly. "Lorcan, we talk every day."

Lorcan stands up from the bench and kneels down in front of me. He takes both my hands in his and rubs his smooth thumbs along the sensitive spots on the back of my wrist.

"Amirah, since your rescue, and especially this past week, you have grown so much. You are kind, funny, and dedicated. You're smart and not afraid to show it." Lorcan pauses.

I'm confused about where this is going, but his words are very sweet. I give him my full attention. Lorcan looks off into the distance, and I can feel his stress.

"What is it, Lorcan? You can tell me anything."

He looks at me and clears his throat. "Anything?" he asks.

I nod, a little afraid of what he has to say. I can't imagine what is making this intelligent, kind, honorable man so stressed.

Lorcan leans in slowly, and I freeze. He places his lips gently on mine, like the brush of a feather--just as soft. He pushes harder, trying to draw me into the kiss. I don't push him away. I don't kiss him back, either.

He breaks the kiss. His cheeks are rosy, and heat rushes up his face. He stands up and walks away. His stiff, retreating back and tense shoulders grow more distant with each step.

Anxiousness fills my heart. He's my friend, and I do not want to lose him.

~

The next morning, after a sleepless night, it's time to meet him for today's lesson.

Lorcan acts completely normal, as if yesterday had never happened. Our strolls in the garden continue to break up our lesson. Our bonds of friendship grow stronger. I don't know why, but when I seek comfort, when I need someone to share my concerns with, it is Lorcan that I turn to. Being with him is like wrapping myself up in a warm blanket by the fire, snuggled in with a cup of tea.

As content as I am when having lessons with Lorcan, I'm relieved that it's soon time for ceremony lessons with Killian. I need his lightheartedness to distract me from the heaviness weighing around my neck, pulling it like a chain. At the window, I pull the curtain aside and stare off into the distance. I hate this. Lorcan matters, and I know I hurt him.

A hand touches my shoulder, startling me. I yelp in surprise and turn to find Killian standing behind me.

"I called you three times, Amirah. Are you okay?"

"Hmm? Yes. Yes, I'm fine. Is it time for our lesson?"

"It is. What say we take our lessons outside today? It's beautiful out."

"Okay," I say and follow him to the door, still lost in thought over Lorcan.

Killian takes the path to the gardens, and my feet falter. I really don't want to be there. I won't be able to *not* think about Lorcan.

"Killian, can we walk somewhere else today?"

He looks at me in askance. He's well aware that the gardens are my favorite place to be. I don't answer his silent question.

He places my hand in the crook of his arm, and we climb the hills. While we are doing so, he quizzes me on the pack ceremonies. At the top, we stop and look out at the vast ocean. Spouts from whales can be seen in the distance. Gray seals and harbor seals lounge on stacks.

Killian guides our conversation. The most mundane topics are funny when talking with him. I laugh at his jokes and rejoice in the lightness of just being in his presence. Where Lorcan is kind and caring, and Blade is fierce and protective, Killian is *fun*. He can make me laugh when it's the furthest thing from my mind.

I don't know if it's the calming atmosphere or just my need to get this off my chest, but I tell Killian what happened with Lorcan. I shouldn't, and I know it--but I can't seem to stop the flow of words from my mouth. Killian sits in silence, listening with rapt attention.

"He *kissed* you?"

"Weren't you listening?" I hurt, remembering the pain and embarrassment I caused Lorcan. There are so many other ways I could have handled that.

"Of course, I'm listening, Amirah. I guess I'm just shocked."

"Shocked? Why?"

"It just doesn't seem like Lorcan."

I nod in agreement because I know this is true. He matters so much to me. I didn't mean to hurt him….

I am lost in thought when Killian gets my attention in the most playful way and makes me laugh as only he can.

"Tag!" Killian taps my arm lightly and takes off, running through a field dotted with pops of blue color from the wildflowers. Thankfully, I'm in trousers and a tunic instead of a day gown. I chase and run as fast as I can.

When I get close to him, he turns so quickly, I lose my balance. I right myself and continue the chase. I've never played tag before. I've never had a friend or a field where I could run free with reckless abandon.

We both laugh gaily under the heat of the beating sun. The simple innocence of the moment makes both of us feel happy and exhilarated. I near Killian again, and instead of running away, he tackles me to the ground. He slows my descent and holds me between his muscular arms, his body pressed lightly against mine.

Suddenly, I stop laughing. We both stop laughing. He gazes in my eyes with an intensity rarely seen in one so lighthearted. His head lowers toward mine. His lips are so close that his breath is a feather touch, gently caressing my lips. "Amirah," he whispers.

The sound of his voice snaps me out of the moment, and I bolt upright. I push him aside and jump to my feet.

"I'm sorry. I can't. We can't."

I see the stricken look on his face. I am sure that my face mirrors his. Only a week ago, we deplored one another. I say nothing more and flee before I hurt him, too.

I run back to the mansion as fast as I can, stumbling over roots and rocks that dot the hillside. As soon as I enter the door, I call for Emma and Bri. Emma comes running from the back of the mansion where the kitchen is. Bri comes out of the library, a book in her hand. Concern is on both their faces.

"What's wrong?" Bri asks.

"Can you just come to my room? Both of you, please, just come to my room."

I hurry through the halls with both of them following me, whispering to each other. Blade appears in the doorway that leads to the hall of the warriors' quarters. He watches me as I walk past without waving. I feel his eyes on me, and I know I'm being rude--but I can't stop for niceties and proper behavior right now.

In my room, Emma grabs my hands in hers.

"What happen'd to ya? Ya look okay."

She scans my body for signs of injury. Bri stands next to her, twisting her hands.

"He kissed me."

"Killian kissed you?" Bri asks.

"They both did." My voice rises. My exasperation makes my face flush pink.

"Which both ya be talkin' bout?" Emma asks.

"What do you mean, 'which both?' Killian and Lorcan, of course."

Frustration mars my features, and I start to pace. Emma shrugs. Amused at my circumstances, she clucks her tongue at me in that way she has when she's going to say something outlandish--well, outlandish to me, anyway.

"Coulda been Blade. I seen the way he looks at ya."

"Stop it. Blade would never--but Killian and Lorcan, they did. They both did, days apart--and Killian did it after I told him what happened with Lorcan."

"She's right," Bri says. Her voice is soft, tentative. "Blade looks at you in a certain way. Plus, Caleb told me he's caught Blade just watching you. I think he is smitten." She smiles shyly.

"Stop it!"

"How can ya miss how Blade looks at ya? A fire burns in that one, fer sure. He is hot for ya."

"Emma, stop. What am I going to do?"

I look at Emma, then turn to Bri. Why are they both holding back laughter? This is not funny. I walk over to the chair by the fire and sit--then stand back up, too upset to stay seated.

"Well, seems to me some fine shifters want ya. I guess what ya can do is pick one?"

"I don't want that. Emma, you *know* I don't want that. You know why. They are my friends. I don't want to lose them, but I can't *be* with them that way--and I would never choose between the two."

"Three," Emma says.

"That's not funny. Blade has never shown an interest in me, thank the Goddesses."

"Yes, he has. I've known Blade all my life, Amirah. He has. Plus, Caleb would know. Blade spends most of his free time helping Caleb train so he can climb the ranks as one of Blade's warriors," Bri says. "Trust me. He's half in love with you."

"Listen, luv. Three of the sexiest shifters I eva laid my eyes on want ya. Why are ya complainin'?"

"I think," Bri says in her delicate way, "that the *bigger* problem is that those three, they're best friends. They've been best friends for a long time. If all three of them have feelings for Amirah, and one of them knows about the other, this can create problems." Bri addresses Emma like I'm not standing right in front of her.

"See? See? This! This right here." I fling my arms wildly in the air. "None of this can happen. None of this *should* happen."

"Well," Emma shrugs again as if my life isn't spiraling out of control at the whims of males. Again. "Just pick one and have yaself some fun."

"Is there one of them whose kiss spoke to you? Does one make you happy in your heart? Who do you want to be with?" Bri asks.

"How can you ask me that? They are nothing alike." I pause and think of earlier on the hilltop. "Killian is fun and carefree, and he makes me laugh. I think I forgot how to laugh, but Lorcan... he brings me comfort, and we share a past that keeps me close to my fathers.... He brings me companionship--and none of this matters. We are all just friends."

"What about Blade?" Bri asks softly.

Throwing my hands in the air at their lack of help, I answer her because I know if I don't, Emma will grab ahold of it like a dog does a ham bone. "Blade makes me feel protected. He makes me feel safe. Can we get back to the point?"

"Sounds ta me that ya need to roll 'em all into one, and you'll have yer perfect mate."

"I. Don't. Want. A. Mate," I enunciate slowly and clearly.

"Well, they want *you*. Things are gonna start gettin' fun 'round here."

Emma gets up and heads to the door. "I gotta get back ta work. Ya take some time and think, 'cuz way I see it, yer the one holdin' the cards, an' ya don't wanna fold too soon." She leaves, closing the door behind her.

"She's right, Amirah," Bri chimes in. "You do need to think. Think if there's one who deserves your time, to see if your hearts entwine-- and if there's not, think of how you will let them down gently and without causing problems amongst their friendships." She leans in and brushes her cheek against mine. "I'll be in the library if you need me."

One thing about living in the mansion: word travels fast.

At dinner, Lorcan, Killian, and Blade are all glaring at each other. Tension blankets the mansion as thick as a winter snow blizzard. The room is filled with a silence that Malachi doesn't even attempt to break. Killian has seated himself to my right rather than by his father as he usually does. Lorcan sits at my left. Servants whisper behind their hands as they bring in the serving dishes. Blade is more watchful, rarely taking his eyes off me from where he stands guard by the door, and when he does, it's to throw glares at Lorcan and Killian. Caleb, on the other side of the door, is watching Blade watch me. Even Willow, Warlock, and the pups are subdued where they lay on the floor by Blade.

Lorcan and Killian vie for my attention with their actions. Lorcan pours me mulled wine, refills my water glass. Killian picks up my napkin when it slides off my lap onto the floor. They treat me like I'm incapable of doing these things for myself and try to one-up each other at every turn.

It's like I have become a competition among them, and they are behaving as though I'm the prize in some rivalry that only they're playing. No, I won't have it--but I won't cut them out, either. I can't. They are too important to me.

Disgusted with everything, I excuse myself from the table and retreat to my rooms. I have so much thinking to do.

When darkness falls, I still cannot silence my mind as memories of time spent with each of them slide through my mind like a deck of cards being shuffled. The strain is heavy as I debate with myself until the day breaks. Should I protect our friendships--*all* of our friendships? Or should I allow us the opportunity to see what can become? After what happened, can I ever trust again enough to try?

# CHAPTER 14

*"Just close your eyes and fall. Fall backwards in your mind and tell me who you see catching you. Is it him... or is it me?" -Victoria L. James*

Things are shifting. It's out of my control, and while a part of me wants to stop it, I don't know if I can.

I'm in a relationship with both Killian and Lorcan, and I don't even know how it happened.

Emma is giddy with it and encourages me to behave in the most inappropriate ways, which, of course, I ignore. Bri often looks at me with sadness and then asks about Blade. Really, though, Blade doesn't show an interest--and besides, I don't know what I am going to do with my two males as it is. A third would likely make me insane.

With Lorcan, it's a type of companionship that a part of me needs. A part of me craves the comfort that he provides. It's like we intrinsically entwined our souls to one another long ago, and it's an unbreakable bond.

Killian and I have moments where I rejoice in a laughter that I never knew I was capable of. He brings out a playfulness in me I never got to experience when I was a child. He has only dared to kiss me on my cheek but takes every opportunity to touch me, even if it's just having me lean against his muscled chest.

They both are so important to me. I have feelings for them. I don't want to, but I do.

I have feelings for Blade, too. He is brutally honest with me. He pushes me to be better, to do better, and I need that. His passion for protecting me and his dedication to the pack are so fierce that I can't help but admire him. His powerful physique is an overwhelming temptation for me. I've caught myself wanting to rub my hand along his bulging biceps.

I don't want to mate with any male. I know I can't completely trust another with my heart--not the way they deserve. But they have become such an integral part of who I am becoming. They hold a piece of my heart. I know I can never risk losing them.

The day has been heavy with my thoughts, but I have been looking forward to starting my combat training. Now that the evening hour is upon us and the training field has the golden glow from the setting sun cast upon its dirt-packed ground, I feel trepidation--not to begin the training, no. It is my duty to defend my pack. I feel trepidation because Lorcan and Killian are going to observe, putting them in close proximity to each other. Outside of meals, this is something I try to avoid.

After Bri's push for me to consider Blade, I paid attention. He watches me constantly. It's likely because he takes his duty as my protector so seriously. Lorcan and Killian are mad at each other when it's *me* they should be mad at. Anytime they are in the same room, everyone stands on pins and needles, waiting for them to go at one another. There's now a chasm between the three, a chasm that hurts my heart to see. It hurts even more to know that, for at least two of them, I am the reason.

Pushing these thoughts aside, I step out on the battlefield, ready for whatever Blade has in store for me. I look behind me to the observation area to check on Lorcan and Killian. They are standing apart from each other, anger across both of their handsome faces.

"Amirah, you need to pay attention to me, not them. If you don't, you can get hurt," Blade says.

"I'm sorry." I turn my attention back to Blade. He's right.

"If it weren't for Malachi basically ordering it, they wouldn't be here. If they become too much of a distraction to you, Amirah, I will order them to leave."

He straps a belt around my waist and puts a pearl-handled dagger in its sheath. He looks up at me, his body so close to mine that his earthy smell overwhelms my senses. My stomach tingles.

"I'll order them to leave now if you want me to."

"No, it's fine. I won't get distracted. I promise." The last thing I want is for more discord between them.

Blade teaches me how to get my dagger out quickly and strike. He pushes me back, makes me gain ground on my own. He uses his body to disarm me or to make me lose my balance.

Sweat runs down between my breasts in pools. My hair is a tangled mess falling out of its long braid. Muscles I didn't even know I had are strained, pushed to their limits of exertion. He is relentless.

We work on pivotal movements, my arm swinging the dagger at Blade. He blocks every move I make as easily as one would swat a fly. I need to try harder. I need to be worthy. I grip the smooth handle firmly in my hand, and I strike again and again.

I know Blade is holding back, but I feel powerful when the blade swipes across his arm. He has his leather and steel training cuffs on, so he is uninjured. *Yes!* I got him. I am too busy celebrating my success to notice Blade bend his knee into the side of mine. I fall to the ground with a thud. In a flash, he disarms me and stands above me, his shadow a dark cloud on my success.

"There's no time in battle for celebrations, Amirah. Even if you lay your opponent down, there can be another behind you or many coming for you from multiple directions. You must think quickly, move faster, and learn to use your senses. You should have known I was going to move before I did. In wolf form, it is even more important. You must learn this now. "

"What the hell was that?" Killian's voice roars from behind me.

I turn to see Lorcan jumping over the railing of the observation deck, his face red with fury. Killian is flying across the battlefield in a fit of rage. I jump to my feet as quickly as my aching muscles allow.

Killian reaches us in a flash and jumps between Blade and me. He shoves his finger into his chest, and his face is inches from Blade's.

"What the hell was that?"

All the goddesses, this is *insane*--but before I can intervene, Lorcan is here. He circles Blade slowly, like a wolf stalking its prey. He's angry. I can see it; I can feel it. Killian is threatening Blade, trying to goad him into a fight. Lorcan is circling slowly, his eyes narrowed and focused, waiting to strike.

"Stop it *right now*. All of you."

"'*All* of you,' Amirah?" Blade looks at me. He's not concerned about taking his eyes off of them and focusing on me. After all, he trained them. He knows what they will do before *they* know. He's the gamma. "I'm doing my duty to train you. These two are the ones who need to stop--and they need to do so before I no longer find them amusing."

Blade looks at Lorcan with a smirk and barely acknowledges Killian standing right in front of him.

"They need to leave my training field, *now*, before I throw them out of it." The smirk turns to a sinister smile.

I take a step back, shocked at seeing such an expression cross the face that has been haunting my dreams for the past few nights.

I appeal to Lorcan. He's the most sensible. The one thing I never wanted to happen is unraveling in front of my face. I am helpless to stop it.

"Lorcan," I say his name. It does not distract him from watching his prey. He stares at Blade with an intensity that is frightening. His muscles are tightly coiled, waiting for the opportunity to strike. Killian shoves Blade, still yelling, hot with temper. Blade barely stumbles. Who *are* these males?

"That's one, Killian, and you get it only because I respect your father. You won't get another."

I have had enough. I yell for Lorcan again and deliberately shove myself between them. Lorcan will not allow them to fight over me and risk me being harmed. Lorcan grabs Killian and pulls him away from Blade. He tries to calm him. Thank the goddesses, Lorcan acted as I suspected. I don't move away from Blade, afraid that if Killian gets away from Lorcan, it will start all over again.

Blade looks at me, and he is no longer amused. He looks at me with disdain and maybe even disgust.

"Next time, Amirah, leave your toys at the mansion. They are no longer welcome in my field." He unsnaps his cuffs. "We are finished for today. I'll let you know when we next train."

He casually walks off of the field, his back straight, his demeanor typical of a gamma. I finally look at Lorcan and Killian, who are now arguing with each other.

"I can't believe you--either of you. I don't need protection."

Killian opens his mouth to speak, but I don't allow it. "I know things are confusing right now. But this--" I gesture widely to encompass the entire field.

"You are *friends*. I will not be the reason you aren't anymore. You can accept things as they are, or it can end, but the issues you all have with each other? Figure it out."

I remove the belt, not looking at either of them. Turning on my heel, I leave them standing there side by side.

I need to go find Blade. My body aches too much for me to catch up with him, but I know he's going to the mansion. I'll catch him before he gets to the warriors' quarters.

At the mansion, I hurry down the hall and catch sight of him just ahead.

"Blade!" I call out.

He ignores me.

"Blade, stop. I have something to say."

The anger on his face is only a representation of the fury that lies below the surface.

"You may have something to say, Amirah, but I have no desire to listen. I don't know what game you are playing with them, but it's beneath you."

Before I can say another word, he enters the warriors' quarters, and the lock clicks. I hate that sound. It takes me back to being trapped in Tiernan's tower.

I lower my head to avoid eye contact with anyone and hurry to my room. I go straight to the window and watch the path that leads from the battlefield for any sign of Lorcan and Killian.

My door slams open. I assume it's Emma or Bri, and I don't want to deal with them as I struggle with my shame and worry. Blade's right. This… *thing* with Killian and Lorcan, it is beneath me. For me to come between two lifelong friends is unacceptable. I didn't intend to, but it has happened all the same.

"Amirah." His voice is a gravelly whisper.

I spin around and face Blade, shocked. He looks so upset that I have to fight the urge to soothe him.

"Amirah, I am sorry. You owe me no explanations. You owe me nothing."

"Why does it bother you so, Blade? I cannot help how I feel, and I didn't want nor ask for their attention. I cannot choose between them; I cannot choose at all."

"I know," he says. Sadness makes his pupils darken and, for the first time since the day I met him, he looks vulnerable.

"Blade, do you want me?" I ask. Why did I ask that?

"What I want does not matter, Amirah."

"It matters to me."

He reaches his long arm out, wraps his hand around my waist, and pulls me to him. I jump at his unexpected actions. My stomach rolls as if a swarm of bees is buzzing in it.

"What I want truly doesn't matter, Amirah. Not to anyone. I am beneath your rank. I'm nothing but a foot soldier compared to you. But should you have any doubt…?"

He runs his hand up my side, and I tremble. He steps closer into my space. His muscular hands grasp my face, and he grazes a thumb along my lower lip. He lowers his lips to mine and whispers, "Just once. I need to taste you just once."

His lips touch mine gently at first, then harder, with the reckless abandon of unleashed passion. I reach up and grab both of his wrists with my hands and sink into the kiss. In my heart of hearts, I have wanted this.

He lets out a low groan and pushes me away. We are both visibly shaken. His moody eyes roam from my face down my body, then back up again. I shiver at the electrifying passion he exudes.

"Never doubt it, Amirah. But it cannot be." He reaches for the doorknob.

"Blade, please."

He pauses, his eyes searching mine, and he finds the desire I have for him. A low growl sounds from his throat, and he turns the lock on the door. This time, the sound doesn't bother me.

He grips my face with his right hand and lays his left on my hip. I lose myself in the depths of passion I see in his eyes. He slowly backs me up. Like a dance, each step is intentional until my back hits the wall. Then time stands still.

"Are you sure, Amirah?"

"I am sure."

My words unleash a primal need in both of us. Blade runs his hands down the length of my arms and snaps them above my head. He shackles both of my wrists in one of his powerful hands, still holding them above me. His lips devour mine, and I am overcome with a need that I didn't know was possible.

I open my mouth wider to allow our tongues to entwine in an intricate motion. I can feel his bulge and arch so that I push into him. He lets go of my waist and grabs the front of my tunic. With a jerk of his hand, he tears it off.

He lets go of my wrists, and I wrap my arms around his neck to anchor myself in this whirlwind of primitive sensuality. He lifts me off the ground with one hand so that I am sitting in his palm. I wrap my legs around his waist. He breaks the connection between our lips but pulls me tighter against him.

I rain kisses along his lips, his neck, and he moves us to the bed. He lays me gently on the bed, one of his hands on each side of my head, and leans over me. After what seems like minutes of staring deep into my soul, he reaches for his trousers and slides them off in one quick motion.

He takes my breath away.

# CHAPTER 15

*"Sorrow is knowledge, those that know the most must mourn the deepest, the tree of knowledge is not the tree of life." -Lord Byron*

I awaken alone in my bed, cold and disappointed that Blade is no longer next to me. My muscles are sore from battle. I'm sore in my intimate places from losing my maidenhood, too.

I carefully get out of bed and stretch my aching body. My door hits the wall with a loud '*thwack*.' Without checking to see who it is, I grab the duvet off the bed and wrap it around myself.

"You got some explainin' ta do," Emma says.

Her voice ricochets in my eardrums like a bullet, and I wince. "What do you mean?"

"Blade flagged me down this mornin' and asked me ta give ya this."

She waves a sealed letter in her hand. I reach for the letter, my chest thumping. She pulls it out of my reach.

"Not so fast," she says. Her lips widen in a knowing smile. "I wanna know what happen'd."

"Just let me read it first, in privacy. Then you and Bri can come in, and I'll tell you everything."

"Everything?"

"Yes, now give it to me."

Emma hands me the letter. "I'll be comin' back before lunch." She exits as quickly as she came.

I lower myself in the chair by the fire and wrap the comforter tighter around me. I take a deep breath and break the wax seal on the letter.


*My Beloved Amirah,*

*Early this morning, I heard some disturbing news, and now I must go on a quick mission. I wish I could say goodbye in person. I owe you that. You have given me a gift more beautiful than you will ever know. I will forever be honored.*

*As I said last night, I know we cannot be. Lorcan or Killian is much more suited to your rank. My heart is heavy as I write this, for I know it is you who I will always love.*

*I will keep you safe and love you from afar. Be happy, Amirah.*

*Forever Yours,*

*Blade*


A sob escapes my throat. The comforter wrapped around me smells like him. His earthy scent makes me more heartbroken. Heedless of my aching body, I throw clothes on and flee the memories of last night.

The cliffs don't bring me the solace I had hoped, but I cannot yet return to the mansion. I escape every second I can because everywhere I turn, I see Blade.

For days, I wander the cliffs, the hillside, the beaches, and the coves. I even haunt the battlefield, hoping to hear news about the mission.

I scold myself for being this upset, but I am helpless to stop it. This hurts more than Tiernan's betrayal had--not because Blade hurt me worse. A more honorable shifter likely doesn't exist. It hurts more because we both have deep feelings and can't or won't do anything about it.

I'm worried, too. There have been whispers from the servants that Blade intends on battling Tiernan himself. To lose him would be more than I can take. I know Blade will protect me from Tiernan with his dying breath, and I know all too well how ferocious Tiernan can be.

Killian has pulled away from me. I don't believe it's because of what happened between Blade and me, but maybe it is. Oh, he still makes me laugh--or tries to. Maybe that's the problem. I am not myself right now. Even Willow is giving me space.

Boots scuffle on the cliffs, and I turn to find Lorcan making his way to me. I wanted to be alone, but if it's not to be, then I am glad that it is Lorcan who is here.

"Emma and Bri have been looking for you. I thought you may be here." He pulls a blanket out of a sack and lays it on the ground. "Come. Sit on this."

I slide onto the blanket. Lorcan sits beside me and casually drapes his arms around my shoulders. He pulls me close. "Just let it out; you'll be better for it." Unable to fight it anymore, I hiccup. My body jerks. Then the tears fly free.

After what seems like an eternity, I stop crying. I am out of tears, my throat burning from the torrent of emotions that pours out of me. Lorcan places his fingers under my chin and raises my eyes to meet his.

"Do you really care so much more for him than me?"

I'm startled by his question. He can't possibly think that, can he?

"Of course not. It's just--it's different."

"Different how?"

"Please don't make me do this right now. You don't understand."

"What I understand is, Blade left early in the morning a fortnight ago after staying with you all night. He didn't say goodbye, but he left you a letter."

My mouth drops open. "My dear, the servants know everything that goes on in the mansion. If you want to know something, you only need to ask. Now close your mouth." He taps my jaw closed.

"I also understand, Amirah, that it is me that is next to you right now. Not Blade. Not Killian. *I* am the one that's here for you. Am I not good enough for you?"

"Lorcan," I say as I grab his arm, "our lives are connected, our friendship, well--" I shrug. "It's kismet. I can't risk losing you. That's what has held me back since you kissed me in the garden."

"Yes, I remember you holding back quite well."

"You don't understand, Lorcan. I *need* you. You are such an important part of my life. I need my best friend."

"What makes you think that if we... moved further, that you would lose me?"

I don't get the chance to answer. Lightning cracks over the sky. When did the weather change? Before I can express concern, the sky opens, and a drenching rain hammers down on us.

Lorcan jumps up, pulling me up with him. He snatches the blanket off the ground and puts it in his mouth. He shifts, his torn clothes on the soaked ground. Helpless to do anything else, I shift, too. He races toward the shelter of the nearest cave, tucked in deep from the winds. I'm close behind.

Inside the cavernous cavity of rock, we both shake the water from our sleek coats. Goddesses, he is so beautiful in wolf form. He exudes a confidence and strength I rarely see when he is human. His coat, his eyes, his muscled body--my heart races.

Lorcan shakes once more, then shifts back to human. He turns his body away, so I only have a view of his back. The muscles ripple with his movement. I let my gaze roam from his back down his body.

He tears the blanket in half and wraps one piece around his waist. He tosses the other half over his shoulder at me. It's drenched, but it's something.

"Go ahead, Amirah. I won't look."

I shift to human and quickly wrap the blanket around my torso, sarong style.

"You can turn around now."

He turns, and together, we walk to the cave's entry and look out at the storm that is attacking the world.

"That was unexpected. Looks like we may be stuck here for a while," he says as he takes in the darkened sky cast over the ocean. "Come, let's talk."

I sigh loudly on purpose, to convey to him I really don't want to. He ignores my hint and sits on the cave floor, leaning casually against the wall. He opens his right arm wide.

"Come on. I'll keep you warm."

Since there's nowhere I can go to avoid this, I concede to his request and curl up in his arm. I am immediately soothed when his warm body surrounds me in comfort.

"So, you and Blade, huh? I guess I can at least be happy it wasn't Killian."

"Stop that. You are all close friends. It needs to stay that way."

"Explain to me what's in your heart, Amirah. I don't want to talk about Blade or Killian. I want to talk about what's in here." He taps my chest with two fingers.

We sit in silence for some time. Patience is a virtue that Lorcan has in spades. He doesn't push. Unable to take the silence anymore, I concede and talk about us.

I tell Lorcan how much I value him as a person. He makes a sound of disgust, but I quickly continue, lest he thinks that's all there is. I tell him why I couldn't give in to the kiss. My fear of losing him when I need him is stronger than my need to have him as my own.

I curl into him more, needing his closeness as much as I need my next breath. I rub my hand on his chest to match the motion of his hand on my back. Our combined movements create a hypnotic state, and the world around me clouds. It's like I'm in a daydream. I feel empowered by his reaction to my touch and giddy with a confidence that astounds me.

Feeling brave and unable to deny whatever this is any longer, I trail my fingers up his bare chest and along the side of his neck, then back down again. My nails brush along his jawline slowly, my touch a bare whisper. He groans, drawing my attention to his face.

We look deeply into each other's eyes. Lost within his gaze, the intimacy between the two of us reaches a level beyond anything I have dreamed of. The boundaries I have put in place to protect our friendship are long forgotten as our essence joins. Overwhelmed by the power I have to control his reactions, I take only a second to ask him what's most important to me.

"Promise me, Lorcan. Promise me I'll never lose you."

He grabs my wrist, stopping me from exploring more.

"I'm not going anywhere, Amirah. I will remain by your side for as long as you will have me."

"No matter what?"

"Amirah. Nothing can drive me away except you telling me to go."

I close my eyes and allow the relief to wash over me. Lorcan slowly lowers me to the ground, careful to cradle my head in his hand. He kisses my eyes, my neck with deliberate attention. He unties the knotted blanket at my breasts and devours my body with his eyes. I can feel his member at the 'v' of my legs when he presses against me, rolling in a sensual motion.

I can't hold back the desire any longer, and I try to pull him inside me, but he is in no hurry. His lips move down my body between my breasts, down my rib cage, and to my navel. He runs his hand from my hip and down the back of my thigh. He lifts my leg to his shoulder and turns his head to kiss the back of my knee.

My eyes roll back in my head as I try to take in the many feelings that zing through my body. I yearn to feel him inside me. His tongue trails along the inside of my thigh, and he breathes deeply, absorbing my scent. He moves above me, my leg still on his shoulder.

"You are perfect, Amirah. I need you as you need me. Never send me away."

Then with slow, deliberate rolls, he teases me--once, twice, then he gives in to desire and enters me.

*"Of all the hardships a person had to face, none was more punishing than the simple act of waiting." -Khaled Hosseini*

Days tick by in slow motion. The servants whisper, and their fear is palpable, yet no one knows anything. I ask Caleb, who says he knows nothing, with a slight tremor in his voice. I look out the library window, watching--always watching.

Lorcan enters. I don't need to look to know it is him. When Killian is around, I feel it, too. Though there is a certain distance between us, I still adore our growing relationship. Were it not for him, I think I would have forgotten how to smile over these long weeks of waiting.

Lorcan places his hand on my shoulder, and I lean back and rest against him and grip his hand tightly.

"I'm worried about him, too. We all are."

"Tension in the mansion is thick. I'm afraid, Lorcan."

"Amirah, Blade has never lost a battle. He is fierce, he is fearless, and he is smart. He's okay. I know he is. If he weren't, I'd know it. We've been as close as brothers most of my life."

I nod my head in acknowledgment and swallow the knot in my throat.

"You must get ready for tonight's celebration. Do you want me to send Emma or Bri up?"

"I don't think we should celebrate anything, but I know it is part of our duty. I hope it just goes fast." I run my hand up his arm. "Their help is unnecessary." I rise on my toes and brush my lips against his. "Thank you."

"For what?"

"For being you--and for understanding."

I hurry to get ready. After I tidy my hair and don a gown as dark as the night sky, I carefully put on my crown. The amulet lays in its bed of crushed velvet, ready for me. It calls to me with its soft, blue glow. I reverently pick it up, and I pray for the goddesses to bring Blade home safe. I lift the amulet to my lips. I put it on and give one quick glance in the mirror, then head to the ballroom.

I see Killian standing at the door. He's so adorable standing there with that wicked grin. His eyes light up when he sees me. Formally, he bends at the waist and bows, then reaches his hand out to me.

Laughing, I run to him and place my hand in his. He lifts it to his lips, then leans his forehead to mine. He tickles me along my rib cage, making me giggle. He brings me such joy.

"Hey, gorgeous," he says with that cocky grin I adore so much. He escorts me through the door, and the pack lines up in rows on either side of the red runner. Though they bow when we walk past, the emotional strain has taken its toll.

I am the Chosen, so it is my duty to say the prayer to the goddesses. I think we all pray a little harder today. We honor Morrigan, the goddess of battle, with gifts of wine, honey, and berries. We gift flora to the other goddesses.

I end the ceremony and release everyone to celebrate, thankful that it's over. I dance for hours; I lead the reels and partner both Loran and Killian.

This time, I don't step on Killian's toes. He exudes a confidence that I admire and switches the steps up to make me laugh. He tickles me in spots that only he knows of, and I appreciate his efforts, though I know this is hard for him, too. The entire pack is trying hard to celebrate, but we cannot appreciate the moment.

"Come, everyone, I have a game," Killian says. He is trying hard to keep spirits high. He's more valuable to this pack than he realizes-- more valuable to *me*.

The pack crowds around him, myself included, Lorcan by my side.

"The name of the game is Impromptu Romance. This is how it goes..."

He explains the rules of the game, in which the 'starter' assigns characters to shifters. Then, they will begin telling a romantic story. When they mention a character's name, that person has to take over the story, and so on.

The story is more and more absurd with each new storyteller. It's nice to hear laughter, but I can't partake in it. Quietly, so I don't disrupt the game, I excuse myself to Lorcan and Killian and go out on the balcony.

The balcony has stands of startlingly bold colors with hurricane candle lamps on top. A large cushioned chaise lounge is in the corner. I sit down and curl my knees into my chest. I wrap my arms around my knees and rest my chin atop with my eyes closed.

"Amirah."

I look up to see Killian walking across the balcony. I knew he was there when I heard the door softly open. Lorcan peers out the door, concern written on his face, and then disappears. Killian climbs behind me on the chaise and pulls me back against his chest, stroking my hair.

"I have a story. Do you want to hear it?" he asks.

I nod my head.

Killian tells me a ridiculous story of a young girl who has mishap after mishap. The dialect that Killian inflicts on her character makes me roll my eyes and laugh out loud. When the story concludes, Killian presses his lips on the back of my neck and the back of my ear, and my female bits stir. I went from laughing to hot molten fire in seconds.

I turn in his arms and press my lips on his.

"I am the last, but I won't be forgotten," Killian says roughly.

He scoops me up and turns me to face him. He grabs the skirt of my gown and pulls it up around my waist. I straddle him and press down against him. He reaches up and pulls pins from my hair, letting the length of it fall down my back and on my shoulders.

The rough material of his trousers rubbing against me creates friction that makes me gasp with each press and roll. The sensual dance makes me whimper in need. He tangles his fingers in my hair and pulls me closer.

"I can't wait," he says.

I rise on my knees so he can reach between our bodies to release himself. His manhood springs free, and he quickly guides it inside of me. We meet stroke for stroke, and I bite down on my lip. Killian whispers words of love and beauty and groans each time he is deep. In seconds, my vision blurs, and my insides explode.

After, I lay in his arms. I know Killian is the least confident of my males. He tries to hide it, but I know it in my heart. I tip my head up, nip his chin, and reach my arm to pull his lips to mine.

"Never last, and never forgotten. You're too important to me," I say.

Relief flashes in his eyes, and he pulls me closer in his arms. We lie in each other's arms and watch the stars twinkle in the sky for some time.

The balcony door crashes so hard, glass shards scatter the ground.

"It's Blade," Caleb says. He turns, running so fast he's a blur of color.

I jump out of Killian's arms, straighten my gown, and run for the door. Killian lifts me from behind and carries me through the glass, then sets me down on my feet. Excitement and uncertainty fill the ballroom as shifters wonder what is going on. I quickly search the room for Lorcan or Malachi. I don't see either of them.

Killian grabs my arm and pulls me to the door. "The council room," he says.

Out of breath and scared, I grab the handle and fling the door open.

# CHAPTER 17

*"Vengeance is in my heart, death in my hand, blood and revenge are hammering in my head." -William Shakespeare*

I see Blade's broad back in the center of the room, and relief washes over me. He's alive. Whatever else is going on, he's alive.

I take a moment to thank the goddesses then rush into the room, my skirt swirling around me. Lorcan stands at his side. The rest of the councilmen, as well as Caleb, surround him.

"Blade," I say loudly to be heard over everyone talking. He turns at his name.

I gasp at the sight of his face and cover my mouth in horror. My knees weaken, and Killian wraps his arm around my waist to give me support. Blade's face is bruised and bloody, and a jagged gash runs the length of his cheek. He has a bloody tear on his throat right beside his jugular. Healing has already started, but it's bad enough that I can't imagine the amount of agony he is in.

I push past Malachi and reach up to cup his red and purple cheek in my hand. The color is fading fast, thankfully.

"Tiernan?" I ask.

He hears the tremble in my voice, and his eyes lock on mine.

"Tiernan and Eamon," he says.

Lorcan clears his throat. "I know you two need a few moments, but we have to know how much time we have before they arrive on the Island. We have to get ready."

Killian moves next to Lorcan. This is the first time I have seen him this serious.

"Days--at best," Blade answers. He turns to Caleb. "Take two warriors from our blue rank and head out to scout. The more notice we have, the better chance we have at beating them."

Caleb moves to the door.

"Caleb," Blade says.

"Sir?" Caleb stops to look at his mentor.

"Be smart. Remember all you've been taught."

A serious look crosses between them. Caleb salutes Blade and hurries to fulfill his orders.

I face everyone. "I know the seriousness of this--more than any of you--but they aren't here right now, and Blade needs to heal before infection sets in. Let him retire to his quarters, and we can reconvene later this evening."

Malachi agrees, and shifters depart the room. Only Blade, Lorcan, Killian, and I remain.

"He tore your throat--in wolf form. He meant to kill you," I say.

Blade's honesty is one thing I know I can always count on.

"He did--he and Eamon both. I harmed them, but as soon as they heal, they will come. I know this. I can feel it."

No one questioned Blade. As Gamma, he senses danger to the pack long before we do.

"I'm going to my quarters now, but I'd like to talk to you two"--he looks at Killian and Lorcan one by one--"before the meeting tonight." He leaves the room.

I run to the doorway and grip the frame, desperation in my every movement.

"Blade!" I yell.

He turns stiffly and looks deep into my eyes. I place my hand on my heart, not breaking eye contact. His rigid stance and emotionless expression bring panic to the fiber of my very being, but I will not look away. After a moment, a smile cracks his lips, and relief washes over me. He places his hand on his heart and bows slightly, then turns sharply on his heel to leave.

It's only this second I notice Killian and Lorcan stand in the doorway, witnessing our interaction. Killian looks hurt, and Lorcan looks resigned.

I'm not dealing with this right now. I rise on tip-toes and kiss first Killian, then Lorcan, and I take my leave to check on Bri.

Later, I leave a petrified Bri in the hands of Emma and try to find my males--all three of them. I am shocked when I hear their voices coming from the parlor. I put my hand on the door to enter, but Killian's words stop me. I press my ear to the door to listen more clearly. Willow and Warlock have taken the pups away, likely to avoid the strain that permeates the air around us.

"I think she needs to choose which of us she wants to mate with."

"She won't choose," Lorcan says.

"Well, she needs to. Look at us," Killian growls. "Lorcan, you are like the walking wounded anytime she is not by your side. And Blade, you can be one nasty gamma when provoked, but you are always on edge now. Your own men avoid you."

"And of you, Killian?" Lorcan says. "You prefer when she is by your side, as well--and when you know she's with me," he continues, "you act like a toddler."

"Enough," Blade interrupts. "She will not choose amongst us. I tried to step away. I know I am beneath her."

"Stop that shit," Killian says.

Blade holds up a hand to stop the conversation from shifting.

"I tried because I know that either of you is more suited, but I cannot. So, you can ask. She will refuse to choose, then each of us has a decision to make. I feel that she is holding something back; we need to know what it is."

I don't want to hear anymore. I step away from the door, thoughts of them ending things tearing at my already damaged heart. I hide in the sunroom, trying to think of the best way to handle this. It is there that they find me.

They enter the room one after the other.

"We need to talk," Killian says.

"He needs to talk; I'm just here to listen." Blade shrugs.

"Sit down, Amirah," Lorcan says softly. Ever the gentleman, he guides me to a chair. His hand brushes along my back as he moves to a seat near where Blade casually lounges.

I look at the three of them, my males. They are so very different, yet they are a powerful, handsome lot. My heart nearly pounds out of my chest in fear that they will force me to choose when I can't.

Killian opens his mouth to speak, and my stomach clenches. I know what he will say, and I cannot--I *will not* choose.

A blood-curdling scream echoes outside the door, preventing Killian's questions. We rush into the hall, and I skid to a halt at the sight of Bri kneeling over a body. Blood soaks her hands and trickles off of her fingertips. I rush to her and pull her away.

Young Caleb lies on the floor covered in blood. His face is pale, and his body shakes with tremors from the substantial blood loss. He is still breathing, but only barely.

I pass Bri to Lorcan and Killian. Blade and I lean over Caleb, taking stock of his wounds. They tore his neck open, but that's not what is killing him--he has a bullet wound in his chest. The hole already shows signs of decaying skin and poison from the silver that is traveling through his body at a rapid pace. He will not survive.

Caleb wheezes words we can't understand through the blood bubbling out of his mouth. Blade takes his hand and leans his ear closer. I know my eyes mirror the pain I see in Blade's. Lorcan pulls Bri into his chest to prevent her from watching Caleb struggle.

Time is running out, and Caleb's life energy slowly seeps from his body. He tries to speak again and chokes on the blood. I gently lift his head and cradle it in my lap.

Blood slides out of the corner of his mouth. "He's here... killed Malachi." He gags again, and I lift his head higher. I quickly glance at Killian to see if he heard what Caleb said. He did not.

"Outside." Caleb rasps. "Gates."

Blade and Lorcan make eye contact over my head, silently communicating. Lorcan releases Bri from the shelter of his arms. They both raise their heads and howl. The ground shakes; the walls crack. First Blade shifts, then Lorcan. With the speed of a whirling cyclone, they charge for the gates.

I softy sing a song pulled from the recesses of my mind--a soothing rhythm to offer comfort. I don't think I ever heard this song, yet I know every word.

Caleb's eyes glaze over, and his chest deflates, exhaling his final breath. Killian comes over and runs his hands over Caleb's lifeless eyes, closing them forever. He lays a blanket over his body, then pulls me to my feet as memories of Bri and Caleb immerse me in overwhelming sadness.

A fury I have never known surges from my head to my toes, and my fingers tingle.

"He will pay. He will pay with his life."

My voice is filled with so much rage I barely recognize it as my own.

Suddenly, paintings fall off the walls, and the floor violently shakes beneath us.

"Goddesses, hear me now."

I turn in a circle, my arms wide. The brilliant blue rays from my amulet strikes objects with their beauty as I move.

"Hear me when I promise you, I promise all my pack, I will seek vengeance. I will destroy all of Red Blood."

My voice rises in volume and strength. The room shimmers in glistening light.

"I will end them all."

# NEXT IN THE SERIES: ENTANGLED SOUL

**The time of my revenge has come. Together with my mates, I will defeat the enemy pack and avenge my loved ones.**

Under the guidance of my three mates, I train for my role as Alpha of the Dark Moon pack. Despite my new, tender condition, which I keep secret from my mates, I push myself to gain new skills and the respect of my pack.

However, as I plot my revenge against the pack that has wronged us, my biggest fear comes true. Once again I've been betrayed by someone I considered faithful.

With time running out, I know I should tell my mates about my new condition, but I'm not ready. How much I care for Blade, Lorcan and Killian still terrifies me.

Yet when horrible events threaten to tear me and my mates apart, I know we must come together to stand a chance of winning.

**Will we manage to defeat our wicked enemy pack, or will I once again be captured and become a prisoner until the end of my life?**

*Entangled Soul is the second book in the Awakening of the Chosen series, a reverse harem paranormal shifter romance. Don't miss this wild, steamy ride with a badass heroine and her hot three shifters!*

**Coming in May 2022!**

Sign up for Callie's Newsletter now so you can be the first to hear about her new release: https://dl.bookfunnel.com/ovzzd2h3t1

Thank you so much for reading *Feral Deceptions*, and I hope you enjoyed this adventure and have been up and down with Amirah. I had a lot of fun writing it!

In the next book *Entangled Soul*, with the 3 hottest alphas, Amirah plots her revenge against the pack that has wronged them. However, her biggest fear comes true!

It never rains but pours. Before she is ready to face the most cruel man in the world, something unexpected happens to her which makes the situation much worse. Yet when horrible events threaten to tear her and her mates apart, she knows they must come together to stand a chance of winning.

Will she manage to defeat our wicked enemy pack, or will she once again be captured and become a prisoner until the end of her life?

I hope you enjoyed it. If you have a moment, please write a short review for it. As an indie author, this means so much to me when it comes to my books reaching more readers. I personally read all of your reviews, and they give me so much motivation to keep writing. Even a sentence or two helps!

>> CLICK HERE TO WRITE A REVIEW <<

PS. I'll also be so happy if you'd like to stay in touch for my new release, discounts, giveaways and fun stuff!

You can also get a copy of the delicious paranormal romance read filled with magic, forbidden love, and heart-pounding action. You don't want to miss it!

Get the prequel for the series *Angel's Guardians* completely for FREE here:

https://dl.bookfunnel.com/ovzzd2h3t1

Love,

Callie

# ABOUT THE AUTHOR

Callie Stone is an avid writer and her writings give a new vibe to the fantasy and paranormal romance genre.

In high school, she met her hero in a friend who introduced her to the world of the paranormal romance novel, and ever since she has carved a niche for herself in the writing world. She has a knack for merging real history and culture with the fantasy world of imagination and serves the mix in her delightful and enchanting paranormal novels.

What she enjoys most is collecting her thoughts by a window seat with her favorite hot chocolate.

Her books bring readers to a new world of imagination with shifters, magic, and thrills. When she is not engaging with her fans, hiking, or enjoying the ambiance of mother nature, Callie spends time in the company of her lovely children and ever-supportive husband as well as her gorgeous cat at her home in Chicago USA.

Ps. You can follow Callie Stone through her newsletter for her latest updates including freebies, sales info, and every new release! And you'll get several recommendations for steamy fantasy books.

Subscribe here: https://dl.bookfunnel.com/ovzzd2h3t1

9 7 9 8 8 1 1 4 5 8 5 9 2